Red Death Over China

SELECTED FICTION WORKS BY
L. RON HUBBARD

FANTASY
The Case of the Friendly Corpse
Death's Deputy
Fear
The Ghoul
The Indigestible Triton
Slaves of Sleep & The Masters of Sleep
Typewriter in the Sky
The Ultimate Adventure

SCIENCE FICTION
Battlefield Earth
The Conquest of Space
The End Is Not Yet
Final Blackout
The Kilkenny Cats
The Kingslayer
The Mission Earth Dekalogy*
Ole Doc Methuselah
To the Stars

ADVENTURE
The Hell Job series

WESTERN
Buckskin Brigades
Empty Saddles
Guns of Mark Jardine
Hot Lead Payoff

A full list of L. Ron Hubbard's
novellas and short stories is provided at the back.

*Dekalogy—a group of ten volumes

L. RON HUBBARD

Red Death
Over China

GALAXY PRESS

Published by
Galaxy Press, LLC
7051 Hollywood Boulevard, Suite 200
Hollywood, CA 90028

Printed in the United States of America.

ISBN-10 1-59212-364-3
ISBN-13 978-1-59212-364-3

Library of Congress Control Number: 2007903541

Contents

FOREWORD   vii

RED DEATH OVER CHINA   1

THE CRATE KILLER   55

WINGS OVER ETHIOPIA   77

STORY PREVIEW:
THE DIVE BOMBER   103

GLOSSARY   109

L. RON HUBBARD
IN THE GOLDEN AGE
OF PULP FICTION   121

THE STORIES FROM THE
GOLDEN AGE   133

Stories from Pulp Fiction's Golden Age

A ND it *was* a golden age. The 1930s and 1940s were a vibrant, seminal time for a gigantic audience of eager readers, probably the largest per capita audience of readers in American history. The magazine racks were chock-full of publications with ragged trims, garish cover art, cheap brown pulp paper, low cover prices—and the most excitement you could hold in your hands.

"Pulp" magazines, named for their rough-cut, pulpwood paper, were a vehicle for more amazing tales than Scheherazade could have told in a million and one nights. Set apart from higher-class "slick" magazines, printed on fancy glossy paper with quality artwork and superior production values, the pulps were for the "rest of us," adventure story after adventure story for people who liked to *read*. Pulp fiction authors were no-holds-barred entertainers—real storytellers. They were more interested in a thrilling plot twist, a horrific villain or a white-knuckle adventure than they were in lavish prose or convoluted metaphors.

The sheer volume of tales released during this wondrous golden age remains unmatched in any other period of literary history—hundreds of thousands of published stories in over nine hundred different magazines. Some titles lasted only an issue or two; many magazines succumbed to paper shortages during World War II, while others endured for decades yet. Pulp fiction remains as a treasure trove of stories you can read, stories you can love, stories you can remember. The stories were driven by plot and character, with grand heroes, terrible villains, beautiful damsels (often in distress), diabolical plots, amazing places, breathless romances. The readers wanted to be taken beyond the mundane, to live adventures far removed from their ordinary lives—and the pulps rarely failed to deliver.

In that regard, pulp fiction stands in the tradition of all memorable literature. For as history has shown, good stories are much more than fancy prose. William Shakespeare, Charles Dickens, Jules Verne, Alexandre Dumas—many of the greatest literary figures wrote their fiction for the readers, not simply literary colleagues and academic admirers. And writers for pulp magazines were no exception. These publications reached an audience that dwarfed the circulations of today's short story magazines. Issues of the pulps were scooped up and read by over thirty million avid readers each month.

Because pulp fiction writers were often paid no more than a cent a word, they had to become prolific or starve. They also had to write aggressively. As Richard Kyle, publisher and editor of *Argosy,* the first and most long-lived of the pulps, so pointedly explained: "The pulp magazine writers, the best of them, worked for markets that did not write for critics or attempt to satisfy timid advertisers. Not having to answer to anyone other than their readers, they wrote about human beings on the edges of the unknown, in those new lands the future would explore. They wrote for what we would become, not for what we had already been."

Some of the more lasting names that graced the pulps include H. P. Lovecraft, Edgar Rice Burroughs, Robert E. Howard, Max Brand, Louis L'Amour, Elmore Leonard, Dashiell Hammett, Raymond Chandler, Erle Stanley Gardner, John D. MacDonald, Ray Bradbury, Isaac Asimov, Robert Heinlein—and, of course, L. Ron Hubbard.

In a word, he was among the most prolific and popular writers of the era. He was also the most enduring—hence this series—and certainly among the most legendary. It all began only months after he first tried his hand at fiction, with L. Ron Hubbard tales appearing in *Thrilling Adventures, Argosy, Five-Novels Monthly, Detective Fiction Weekly, Top-Notch, Texas Ranger, War Birds, Western Stories,* even *Romantic Range.* He could write on any subject, in any genre, from jungle explorers to deep-sea divers, from G-men and gangsters, cowboys and flying aces to mountain climbers, hard-boiled detectives and spies. But he really began to shine when he turned his talent to science fiction and fantasy of which he authored nearly fifty novels or novelettes to forever change the shape of those genres.

Following in the tradition of such famed authors as Herman Melville, Mark Twain, Jack London and Ernest Hemingway, Ron Hubbard actually lived adventures that his own characters would have admired—as an ethnologist among primitive tribes, as prospector and engineer in hostile climes, as a captain of vessels on four oceans. He even wrote a series of articles for *Argosy,* called "Hell Job," in which he lived and told of the most dangerous professions a man could put his hand to.

Finally, and just for good measure, he was also an accomplished photographer, artist, filmmaker, musician and educator. But he was first and foremost a *writer,* and that's the L. Ron Hubbard we come to know through the pages of this volume.

This library of Stories from the Golden Age presents the best of L. Ron Hubbard's fiction from the heyday of storytelling, the Golden Age of the pulp magazines. In these eighty volumes, readers are treated to a full banquet of 153 stories, a kaleidoscope of tales representing every imaginable genre: science fiction, fantasy, western, mystery, thriller, horror, even romance—action of all kinds and in all places.

Because the pulps themselves were printed on such inexpensive paper with high acid content, issues were not meant to endure. As the years go by, the original issues of every pulp from *Argosy* through *Zeppelin Stories* continue crumbling into brittle, brown dust. This library preserves the L. Ron Hubbard tales from that era, presented with a distinctive look that brings back the nostalgic flavor of those times.

L. Ron Hubbard's Stories from the Golden Age has something for every taste, every reader. These tales will return you to a time when fiction was good clean entertainment and the most fun a kid could have on a rainy afternoon or the best thing an adult could enjoy after a long day at work. Pick up a volume, and remember what reading is supposed to be all about. Remember curling up with a *great story.*

—Kevin J. Anderson

KEVIN J. ANDERSON *is the author of more than ninety critically acclaimed works of speculative fiction, including The Saga of Seven Suns, the continuation of the Dune Chronicles with Brian Herbert, and his New York Times bestselling novelization of L. Ron Hubbard's Ai! Pedrito!*

Red Death Over China

Chapter One

JOHN HAMPTON patrolled the eastern shore of the Yellow River in a way as careless and slipshod as the rickety, ancient Bristol.

The Bristol had wandered in from faraway England, an outcast, and wandered without any destination more definite than old age.

John Hampton was little better than his ship. He had less color to him than the dun plains which reached interminably to the smoky foothills. He was an in-between—he stood for nothing definite, he cared about nothing, he knew nothing he wanted.

Even the puffballs of volley fire on the ground meant little to him. He knew that the southern soldiers did not have enough training to lead him his length. Faintly contemptuous, he looked down at the muddy banks of the Yellow River, and inland to occasional barricades crudely made of bagged sand and piled muck.

Far away, a growing dot against the saffron haze of the day, another plane was coming. It could not be a friend, as the Bristol was the only plane Mao possessed and John Hampton, such as he was, the only pilot.

A fight was in the offing. He knew that and did not greatly care. The Bristol was fleet enough to run away.

Southern soldiers on the ground had seen their ally on the wing. Impulsively they leaped up on their earthworks—bouncing gray dots, something less than human.

Behind John Hampton, a Lewis yammered. He turned and looked at his gunner and shook his head.

The gunner showed no surprise, neither did he show any tendency to obey. He was a wild-eyed little man with uncontrollable black hair which came out from under his oversize helmet and streaked back from his yellow face in the whipping wind.

Chou, the gunner, again depressed the muzzles of the Lewis guns and raked a barricade. He looked defiantly back at the foreign devil in the front pit.

John Hampton shrugged. The Lewis started up again. Leaping puffs of dust sprang up beyond the barricades. Bouncing gray dots scrambled backwards, falling into grotesque, shuddering heaps.

John Hampton looked at the oncoming plane and turned a bend in the stream, his plane's shadow flowing through the depths of the murky water. He could wait a little while. It would look better if he took a burst or two before he went away. Not that he cared whether or not he made any show but, after all, his gunner would talk. As nearly as possible, Hampton stuck to the middle ground of existence.

The other plane was getting big enough to distinguish its type. It was a two-seater, an observation plane, but more than a match for the Bristol.

Hampton cared little about that either.

The rattle of the Lewis guns annoyed him, but it was useless to tell his tail gunner to stop.

The Rolls was cruising and still had a few horses to spare. Hampton kept on his course. There would be nothing to report this day. There was never anything to report. Men died on both sides of the river but they were men in gray cotton and there was nobody to mourn their passing.

General Mao's CPVAJR Army was fighting with its back to the Great Wall and the Sinkiang Desert, outnumbered, out-armed, but not out-generaled. The great Chiang was making one last great push to wipe out his rebel generals forever. And now only the Yellow River's greasy flood intervened. The fanatical troops of Mao were low on food, clothing, ammunition, rifles, horses. . . . But they were holding out at the Yellow River, dying on the wintry plains of Shensi.

The two-seater roared forward into the fray, hungry prop chopping off the distance in a churning blaze of light.

John Hampton squared around in the front cockpit of the Bristol and shoved his throttle full out. The clanking Rolls trembled in its mounts. The ancient Bristol's wings shivered. The patched fuselage angled away.

Chou's twin Lewis guns rattled ferociously and the southern two-seater veered hastily off.

Hampton had taken the burst. Now he could go home. He touched rudder and stick and stood the Bristol around.

The two-seater executed a swift three-sixty. Bow guns going, it clamped itself to the Bristol's tail. Tracer ate up from the rudder toward the gunner's pit, gobbling small round holes which smoked in the slipstream.

Hampton verticaled, cocking his right wing down at the river's yellow face. Chou raked the two-seater from prop to rudder, his wide eyes alight with joy.

But the southern plane was not touched in any vital spot. Pilot and gunner, caring little about an ancient Bristol, swooped away and came back under the Bristol's belly.

Hampton kicked rudder. Chou was almost over the side with his guns. He fired short, rapping bursts downward into the other two-seater's nose.

The Bristol straightened out again. Hampton was once more heading toward his field, away from the river.

The southern ship scrambled for height, went over the hump and streaked down. Chou, leaning back against the rim of his pit, centered his sights on the two-seater's nose and again let drive.

Small round holes, gashed by southern bullets, crept up the tail, inch by inch. Chou held his shaking guns and shouted defiance into the shattered wind.

The holes came inevitably forward. Hampton verticaled away. The two-seater hung on. Chou's words rose to a shrill scream, audible even above the yowl of engines and guns. He was driving his bullets with every ounce of energy he possessed.

The two-seater followed around. Once more the yellow waters were under the Bristol's canted wings. Once more the southern slugs were eating into the Bristol's fabric, rapping steadily forward to the gunner's pit.

Chou leaned into his Lewis guns. His bullets were almost

gone. His target was never in place. But he yelled and defied the southern dogs to try their worst.

The slugs came up the turtleback, smoking as they riveted wood and steel.

Chou's last bullets were chattering out. The two-seater's prop was in his sights. The target was fair, coming straight on for an instant. Chou held on.

The southern slugs passed over the mount, drove black dots into the leather seat, into the floor, into the empty ammunition racks.

The southerner's prop exploded into a fanning pattern of fragments. Smoke swept out from under the two-seater's cowl. Chou was holding on.

The two-seater lurched and dived helpless into the yellow water, sending up a soaring column of dirty spray.

Chou grinned feebly. He raised his hand halfway. It dropped suddenly over the side and Chou sagged over the skyward pointing guns. A small, dark trickle ran out of his mouth and out of his sleeve, to blend together and match the scarlet of the red star on the Bristol's side. Chou grinned again. He coughed and tried to right himself. His head dropped limply to wobble against the bright steel of his gun mounts.

Hampton looked back and saw him. He knew nothing could be done. The two-seater was a scattered patchwork raft floating slowly down with the murky river. The sky was clear. The barricades on the eastern shore were once again dotted with puffs of volley fire. Chou's glazed eyes looked down and back at them, not caring now.

The wind had carried the fight far down the stream, across

many bends of the tortuous course. When Hampton spotted his position he saw that the closest way home was through enemy country.

But the two-seater was gone and even though his gunner was dead, as long as his motor continued to run there was nothing to be feared.

Hampton was shaken. It was a new experience for him. His life was such an even, listless plane. He had seen many men die and he did not really care. But Chou—he had known him. Chou had cursed him day and night, had hammered at him to get the patrols done. Chou had been so fiery and alive. . . . Hampton glanced back at the dangling hand which moved to and fro to smear the red star.

He faced front again and straightened out his course. He was not really thinking. His gray eyes were dull, almost bored. His lean, common face showed no particular strain, even now.

But something he could not define stirred uneasily within him.

They had drifted farther than he had thought. He found himself far east of the bending river, crossing over a wide, deserted plain. It was cold, but in this land it rarely snowed. Dust, bitter, chilly dust, was eddying along the ground. As far as Hampton could see, the horizon was smoky and yellow.

He hunched down in his pit, flying like an automaton, wishing only that he had a drink—and not even ardently about that.

Something was usually doing on this plain, but not today. No troops or trucks marred the gray-brown expanse. Only the dust and the shadow of the ship moved in the sullen world.

Dully Hampton remarked the absence of troops below. He would remember and mention it in his report—after he had a drink. Nothing stirred. . . .

To the north he thought he saw a sparkle of metal in the cold sunlight. Presently it was repeated.

It was one thing to watch in a world of sameness. Hampton watched it.

The sparkle multiplied until black dots could be seen behind them. It was a detachment of cavalry, a southern squadron patrolling behind their lines.

Then Hampton saw that the horses were running and that the Mongol mount in the lead was far ahead of the rest. Too far ahead to be the leader.

He was flying in the same direction that the horses rode. The Bristol's shadow came up and overtook them with a contemptuous flicker, passing swiftly by. Faces jerked up and ponies dashed to the right and the left. They had seen the red star.

But Hampton would not have machine-gunned them. He wanted to go home and take a drink. He looked down at them as he passed.

The single horseman out in front wheeled around and opened his mouth as though to shout. He raised his arm and waved it frantically at the Bristol.

The movement attracted Hampton's flagging attention. Cold and hazy as the sunlight was, thick though the dust, Hampton was not so high that he failed to see a red star on the soldier's cap.

This was odd. Below was one of Mao's officers, deep in

enemy territory, cut away from his troops by the barricades and the river, pursued by southern cavalry.

Hampton glanced back at Chou's dangling arm. Something stirred uneasily within him again. An impulse was as foreign to him as he was to China, and yet something very like an impulse seized him and made him obey.

The Bristol verticaled and came back at the southern troops. Hampton stabbed the nose down and opened up with his bow guns.

The knot of horsemen scattered wildly right and left. A chunky Mongol pony went down. The rider rolled out and lay still. Dust streaked in straight, violent lines through other men and horses, dotting the dun plain with gray and brown.

The man with the red star on his cap was still racing away. Hampton turned and looked again at Chou. He looked down at the earth which was flat and hard. He saw the upraised hand of the officer.

Hampton cut his gun and leveled out. The officer rode wide and Hampton floated the Bristol above the plain. The wheels crumped against the rough earth and the Bristol slowed.

In the comparative silence came the sharp raps of rifles far behind. Horsemen were spurring in pursuit, shooting as they came.

The officer swerved in alongside the still rolling ship.

Hampton shouted, "Throw out the gunner and get in!"

The officer looked at Chou and then at Hampton. Mounted, his head was as high as the pits. There was a strange expression in his eyes.

"Throw out the gunner!" shouted Hampton. "They'll nail us in a second. Snap into it!"

He had never spoken that emphatically before, but that was not the occasion of the officer's stare.

Hampton noticed then that blood was staining the fellow's tunic. A round hole, very dark, was under his breast pocket. The officer looked back at the running cavalry and shook his fist. A bullet ricocheted off the wing and screamed away.

The officer took the side of the cockpit and lifted himself from his saddle. The effort must have cost him agony, but his only expression was one of triumph toward the cavalry.

He came down in the pit beside Chou. The pony streaked away, afraid of the engine's sudden roar. Another bullet splintered a strut before Hampton got away.

The Bristol rolled faster and faster. The cavalry was left impotent, far behind.

The Bristol roared skyward and Hampton looked back. He met the strange look in the wounded officer's eyes.

Chapter Two

MAO'S front line and the picked troops of his CPVAJRA were located very near the Yellow River at the moment, that being the best bar to the advancing minions of Chiang. General headquarters were situated in the City of the Red Pagoda, an old, crumbling town, walled since time began, the scene of eons of struggle between barbarian and Chinese, the north and south, bandits and government.

The town itself had had more rulers than man could remember. Perhaps if the Red Pagoda itself could have spoken, the mystery of the city could have been explained—but not otherwise.

A man whose life and grave had both been swallowed up in time had once built the Red Pagoda. Today its crumbling hulk towers over the walls, rendering them puny by comparison. The curves, eroded by wind and dust, have long since lost their grace. The color has changed to a nondescript dun and only a few of the fallen bricks show flecks of red.

This had been a last stand before—many times before. But never had the town meant so much to a people as it did to the CPVAJR Army. If the City of the Red Pagoda fell before advancing, powerful Chiang, two hundred thousand men would die, a society would disappear from the face of the earth.

The Great Heroic Trek would have vanished, meaningless, into time with the rest of the city's history.

Hampton cared nothing about this. The Red Pagoda was to him only a landmark, the first seen from afar and perhaps a thing which cast its long shadow across the courtyard of his quarters. The shadow was there now, a thin gray thing, laid out by the hazy sun of morning.

Hampton had slept well after his air fight the day before. There was nothing to hinder his sleeping. But his eyes were red-rimmed and his fingers shook a little as he drew on his gloves—not from emotion but from whiskey.

He looked back at his unpainted table and saw the bottle of rice-brew standing there. He shrugged and made a move toward it. The doorway lost a part of its rectangle and he turned to see a diminutive messenger standing there, his face a blank, an envelope in his hands.

Hampton took the letter and read his orders. They were brief:

> Patrol east shore of Yellow River and keep air clear.
> Liang is being assigned to you as gunner.
> Hiao Teh-tung, Colonel

Hampton thrust the letter in his pocket and moved again toward the bottle. He thrust it into his gray jacket and walked out past the messenger without looking at him.

He rounded the corner of a wall and came into the cold sun. A bench was there and on it sat the officer he had picked up the day before.

Hampton started to pass with hardly more than a nod when the man leaned forward a little as though to stop him.

"You do not look well this morning," said the Chinese in cultured English.

"I look all right," replied Hampton.

"Perhaps the strain of too much flying—"

"Strain? Well, no. Not that."

The officer's arm was in a sling and he looked as gray as his cotton tunic. But he smiled. "I have been waiting here to thank you for picking me up yesterday."

"You needn't have bothered," said Hampton. But for the first time in more years than he could recall, he was interested in something. "You look pretty sick. You better get into bed."

"There is too much to be done," replied the officer, still smiling. "You must leave immediately?"

"Pretty soon," said Hampton dully. "I've got to earn my pay."

The officer's fine brown eyes widened a trifle. "I wanted to thank you for saving—"

"That isn't necessary," said Hampton. "I just saw you riding along and I was going the same way. I wasn't even thinking about saving anybody's life."

The officer seemed to know that Hampton was not being modest but, rather, Hampton disliked to talk.

"I didn't mean saving my *life*," said the officer, gently. "I was carrying dispatches and currency. Mao needed them both."

Hampton smiled slightly. It was not a pleasant expression. He looked searchingly at the other, almost on the point of laughter. Hampton had never seen any sense in flag-waving.

15

"No use getting yourself killed for nothing," said Hampton. "Why did you try such a stunt?"

"Someone had to bring them through," said the officer, still smiling.

"What's the difference?" said Hampton. "You didn't have a chance."

"But I got through," said the officer. He changed the subject quickly. "I have not introduced myself, Mr. Hampton. I am Captain P'eng Teh-lai."

Hampton barely nodded.

"I am surprised," continued the captain, "to find an American espousing our cause. I did not know we had one here. We are very fortunate to have an excellent pilot."

Hampton brushed it aside. "A guy in Shanghai asked me to deliver that Bristol. When I got here I didn't have anything else to do and the pay was all right. I'm not interested in any cause. A man's got to do something, hasn't he?"

The captain still smiled. He was handsome, almost as tall as Hampton. But there was a remarkable difference between the men, far wider than the gulf of race.

"You perhaps do not care about our cause?" said the captain.

"One's as good as another as long as the pay is right."

"You have, perhaps, had many causes?"

"Plenty."

"I have heard that you were once in the United States Army."

"Yeah."

"And in the Chaco affair in South America."

"They paid pretty well," said Hampton.

The captain looked strangely at the American. He could

read men very well, could the captain, and he knew definitely in spite of Hampton's tone that money meant nothing to him. The captain was puzzled.

"I still can't see why," said Hampton, "you'd try such a stunt as you did. Didn't you know that plain is patrolled?"

"Yes, I knew," replied the captain.

"And yet you ran the risk of getting yourself killed."

"That is my job," said the captain. "There is something else. . . ." He hesitated and decided not to go on. Abruptly he said, "Do you know the story of that Red Pagoda, Mr. Hampton?"

"No," said Hampton, disinterested.

"Do you mind if I tell it to you?"

"No," said Hampton, dully.

"It is about a youth by the name of Lin and it happened a very long time ago," began the captain. "This city was not then known by its present name. That was changed afterwards so that no one could ever forget.

"It was at the time when the Mongols had driven a deep wedge into China from the north. They seized and burned everything in their path except this city. They intended to hold it as a base from which they could launch offensives deeper into China.

"One Chinese commander and a small body of troops tried to come back and take this city from the Mongols. They were routed with great loss and among the missing was a young officer named Lin.

"He had been captured and he had not been put to death. The Mongol chief had a reason. He knew that the Chinese would gather more troops and come back and he knew that one more defeat would open the broad highway into China. The Mongols were not as strong as they were supposed to be, but this city, manned as it was, could never be taken by storming the walls. It could only be recaptured by the Chinese by siege. Unless a supply train arrived for the Mongols, the Chinese would win.

"That is why Lin was not put to death. The Mongols held him for a week, waiting for their supply train. Finally the Chinese came again from the south.

"The Mongols waited until the Chinese were under the walls and then the Mongol chief ordered that Lin be brought up to the topmost platform of the Red Pagoda and shown to his people.

"The Mongol commander placed a sword against Lin's back and told him what to say. Lin was to shout that the Mongols were well supplied and that immense reserves were coming up to cut the Chinese off. If Lin said this, the Mongols knew that the Chinese would believe him and withdraw, leaving the way clear for the Mongol conquest.

"Lin looked down at the officers in advance of his people and then looked back at the Mongol commander's sharp sword. You can see that the drop from that tallest platform to the ground is almost three hundred feet. Lin looked down at the pavement far below.

"'Speak!' said the Mongol. Lin looked again at his people. He shouted, 'The Mongols have no supplies. Cut off the supply train and they are dead men!'

"The Chinese heard, the Mongols suddenly understood

that they were finished. The commander stabbed Lin and the youth fell from that highest platform to this hard pavement below.

"Lin died. But the Chinese took the City of the Red Pagoda and the Mongols were thrown back to the Great Wall."

Hampton had waited until the captain finished. He was not eager to start his patrol.

"I have bored you," apologized the captain, standing up and smiling.

"That guy was a fool," said Hampton without heat. He glanced at his watch and nodded to the captain. He went out of sight around the end of the gate, walking slowly. Once he glanced back and saw the captain watching him. That was all.

Chapter Three

HAMPTON'S ship had been patched up during the night. It had needed it. The mechanics had rolled it out into the bitter wind and it idled now, the Rolls coughing asthmatically in the chill gray air.

Hampton walked toward it, head down. He did not like the cold and, somehow, for the first time in his life, he did not like himself.

A staff officer was standing beside the wing of the ship, looking like a Buddha idol in his enormous greatcoat. It was the colonel in command of the "air forces."

Hampton would have passed him with little more than a nod but the colonel thrust out his hand to stop him. The colonel spoke English. Like the captain, his education was extraordinary.

"Hampton," said the colonel, "there is something I would like to add to my written orders this morning."

Hampton gave him a disinterested glance, waiting.

"That was a fine piece of work you did yesterday, Hampton," said the colonel. "Without P'eng Teh-lai's dispatches we did not know what course to take in our defense. Thanks to your brilliant rescue of the captain we now know that Chiang's troops intend to throw a pontoon bridge across the Yellow

River, covering it with artillery, and cross during the night. They are even now bringing up the materials—which are not to be found in the vicinity."

"It wasn't anything," said Hampton, uncomfortably.

"It was a great deal," corrected the colonel. "All of us appreciate it. Before we thought we detected a listlessness in you which we found hard to diagnose, but I am glad to find that we were wrong. It took a great deal of courage to rescue P'eng."

Suddenly Hampton snatched at a piece of truth. "It took more courage for Captain P'eng to try to get across that plain." He was faintly surprised at his own heat.

"You are modest," said the colonel.

Hampton felt abashed. There was something wrong here. Something was happening to him against his will. Gruffly he said, "You had some further orders for me?"

"If you would be so kind as to try to carry them out, yes. The mission is dangerous, Hampton."

"The pay's all right," said Hampton.

The colonel took no visible notice of this though it was, in fact, a slap, no matter how unintentional. The colonel, the captain, Mao—they did not fight for pay.

"One of our men," said the colonel, "has been stationed to the south, on the route of Chiang's reinforcements. He will know the strength of Chiang's artillery. That knowledge is vital to us. His house is marked by a red door. It stands alone just at the far edge of the plain across the river, up against the foothills. You could land there, Hampton."

"If that's my job," said Hampton.

22

The colonel was about to speak but he did not.

"Okay," said Hampton.

He climbed up on the catwalk and slid into his pit. His gunner, Liang, was already behind his guns. He was a small, thin-faced fellow. His eyes were very much alive, but he was otherwise without expression.

The colonel saluted and stepped back. Hampton stabbed at the throttle and the Rolls roared.

A fog of gray dust was beaten up from the ground, laying a smoke screen to mark the course of the ship. The Bristol took the air, leveled out and swept eastward toward the Yellow River.

Chapter Four

THE river was a muddy dragon curling its sinuous length from horizon to horizon—a dragon which spat flame from its sides.

The barricades sprawled out along the yellow banks, peopled by gray ants which scrambled up and shook their puny fists at the Bristol.

Chiang had brought only a few planes into the region. It was far from his base of supplies and fuel was hard to get. The CPVAJR Army, after making a running fight of seven thousand miles, was now on the last limit of Chiang's government. But Chiang wanted them. A quarter of a million dollars was General Mao's blood price. The other CPVAJRA soldiers and officers ranged from that down to a few coins. Chiang was here, a quarter of a million strong, to collect his own blood money.

Mao's back was against the mountains, against Inner Mongolia. And now if he could keep his front clear he was safe, in complete control of a province containing hundreds of thousands of square miles, countless millions of people—a province which had hailed Mao's coming, had welcomed his troops. It was not power which Mao and his men craved, but freedom. In their domain the peasants could own their land—a fact which was not equaled in all of China.

Mao's officers died to carry on. When captured they were boiled alive, tortured, burned. If Chiang succeeded in crossing the Yellow River, two hundred thousand officers and men would die. There was no escape.

Hampton knew all this vaguely. He caught himself puzzling over it now. But he did not understand—not yet. He was only troubled. He had glimpsed himself as others knew him and the glimpse had not been good.

Flying over the troop-patterned plain, jarred now and then when Liang opened up on the detachments below, he remembered the story of the Red Pagoda. Why did that bother him?

Neither bad nor good was Hampton. Neither a brave man nor a coward. Neither handsome nor ugly. Neither intelligent nor ignorant.

He saw himself that way and thought about the Red Pagoda.

They had come far. The troops were no longer flicked by their passing shadow. Liang tapped him on the shoulder and he turned.

Liang was pointing down and Hampton's gaze followed the finger. He saw a squat stone house with a faded pink door. That was his destination.

He looked about for a place to land and saw a walled field nearby. It was small but it would do. He looked around the horizon and suddenly saw a detachment of cavalry far off. The troop had stopped, no dust rolled away from them. They could not help but see his landing.

He looked back at the square stone house. He remembered the words the colonel had spoken. With an anger foreign to him, he snapped into the slipstream, "What the hell? The pay's all right!"

He cut his throttle and coasted down the cold stairway of the sky, banking around into the wind. He fishtailed and the wires sang. He pulled back on the stick and the Bristol floated an instant, abruptly settling on the rough earth. He gunned the engine and came around into his own dust.

The motor coughed and clanked to a stop—startling Hampton, who saw that his mags were still on. He lifted himself up in his pit and saw a Chinese sprinting toward the mud fence, shouting as he came. Far off to the right Hampton could see a dust cloud beginning to roll, which meant that the cavalry had spotted the red star on the side of the fuselage.

Hampton turned to Liang and spoke in a strange, tight voice. "The gas line must be choked with this dust. Stick by those guns until I clear it."

Liang blazed with excitement and seized a wrench and began to attack his gun mounts. Hampton stepped out of his pit to his catwalk, drew off his gloves and tugged at the straps on the cowl.

The Chinese vaulted the fence and raced across the field. He came to a panting stop beside the Bristol. Hampton looked down and saw that the fellow was a peasant, clothed in rags. But he did not look like any other peasant Hampton had ever seen. There was something triumphant in his voice, something glorious.

"Chiang's cavalry is coming!" cried the peasant. "We must get away!"

Liang looked at the rolling gray dust and then at the tattered Chinese. "Give your dispatches to this pilot. Quickly!"

The peasant snatched a packet out of his worn jacket and dropped it into Hampton's cockpit. "They are all there. The batteries of artillery, the number of troops, the type of weapons, the amount of food, the time of arrival of the pontoons."

"They must get to the City," said Liang. "Help me."

Liang lifted up his Lewis guns and handed them over the side to the peasant, who nodded to show that he understood and approved.

Hampton, disconnected gas line in hand, looked up and saw what was happening. "Wait! What's the idea? You can't do that!"

Liang faced him from the ground. "There is no time to explain. We will have to stop that detachment from the far side of the field. Otherwise they will shoot you down before you can take off. We will hold them."

Hampton was jarred. "Wait! We'll stand them off together!"

"That would be too big a chance to take," cried the peasant. "Don't you see? Neither Liang nor I can fly this plane. You are the only necessary one of the three. My report must be taken to Mao!"

To save argument Liang and the other Chinese picked up the Lewis guns and ammunition drums and raced out to meet the gathering cloud. They ran very fast, covering the distance between the plane and the faraway mud wall in half a minute. Hampton saw them throw the guns down on their chosen barricade and kneel behind them.

Hampton bent over the gas line and blew into it without noticing the dry flatness of the gasoline. He looked up again. The cloud of dust was almost upon Liang and the peasant now. Hampton disappeared under the cowl again. He heard the Lewis guns open up with a chattering roar.

How long could those guns last on the ground? How long would it take them to freeze?

His hands were shaking when he joined the line to the carburetor, shaking worse when he tried to adjust the crescent wrench. He looked up again. The dust had swallowed Liang and the peasant but the Lewis guns still rapped in short, wicked bursts. A horse screamed in unforgettable agony. A bedlam of curses and a jangle of sabers pierced the bitter air.

Hampton fitted the crescent wrench and tightened up the line. He slid down the fuselage to the cowl, leaned in and threw his switch. He looked up as he opened his throttle. The Lewis guns were still going. Hampton glanced down to his seat and saw the dispatches lying there, nothing but a dirty packet of papers, very still and square.

He dropped to the ground and raced around his wing. He yanked the prop through and heard the gas suck into the cylinders. No time for caution now. He grabbed the club and pulled it into position again. The Lewis guns stopped suddenly.

The sound of pistol shots were loud and sharp.

Hampton felt as though somebody were strangling him. He raced sideways with the club. The Rolls caught. The Bristol shivered and began to trundle forward across the bumpy ground.

Hampton heard the yells behind him and turned to stare for an instant toward the barricade. Through the dust he could see a blurred knot of riders streaking down upon him, sabers at charge.

Hampton grabbed the wing. The Bristol came around at right angles and rocked forward. He jabbed his boot in the stirrup and spilled over the turtleback and into the pit. He opened the throttle wide, shoved ahead on the stick, felt for his trips.

Behind his goggles his eyes were terrifying. His mouth was compressed into a hard, downward curve. His fingers stiffened on the trips.

The Bristol rocketed at the coming group. Hampton's feet alternated on his rudders. The Bristol careened drunkenly from left to right and back again, scraping wingtips in the dust.

A spraying fan of fire blasted out and through the prop. The horses started to veer and were fairly caught. Riders fell into the spurting yellow dust. Plunging, maddened mounts rolled over and over.

All sound was lost in the engine's din.

The Bristol swept between the two squirming piles on the plain and instantly buried them with the blasting slipstream.

Hampton's mouth was harder now. His eyes were like two jets of flame.

The Bristol came off and shot steeply into the sky, away from the dust, the cavalry.

A hundred feet off it did a swift wingover.

Below by the wall the haze was clearing. As it rolled back Hampton could see the muzzles of the Lewis guns pointing silent and twisted at the sky. Beside them, riddled with bullets and hacked by sabers, lay Liang and the peasant.

A startled ring of cavalrymen stabbed agonized looks upward. They divined the Bristol's purpose, jabbed home their spurs and flayed their quirts, striving to clear away from the spot.

Hampton laid the belly of his ship close against the ground. He kicked his rudders. His fingers bent the trips as he pushed them. A fanning blanket of fire flashed outward from the Bristol's nose.

Horses somersaulted. Men reeled back and dropped into the dust. Soldiers stiffened as though on parade and rolled sideways under the thundering hoofs.

An officer whirled and emptied his pistol.

When the Bristol pulled up, the officer was face down, clutching the smoking automatic in his slowly relaxing hand.

Hampton jumped to two hundred feet, put one wing down and went around full gun, looking over the side at the beaten, trampled field.

One lone trooper was spurring into the distance, looking back with terror, coming down again and again with his quirt. He had lost his sword and rifle. He had lost his bravado. He laid low over the horse's neck and sent a prayer to the Great God Bud.

Hampton whipped the Bristol level, turned the other way, put the nose down and streaked across the earth, blasting back the yellow dust as he went.

The trooper looked back.

Hampton closed on his trips.

Hampton whipped the Bristol level, turned the other way,
put the nose down and streaked across the earth,
blasting back the yellow dust as he went.

The horse stood on its head and came down in a skidding pile, lying still.

Hampton zoomed, looked back.

Nothing moved on the barren field but the dust.

When he was far above the earth, heading home, he saw the Red Pagoda, an angular tower against the yellow sky, growing larger as he approached the town.

Chapter Five

WHEN the Bristol stopped rolling, Captain P'eng limped out to meet it, his young, thin body bent with the pain it cost him.

Hampton sat in his pit looking back at the city. His eyes were above the level of the walls. He did not speak when P'eng drew near.

Neither did P'eng speak. He turned and followed the direction of Hampton's eyes and saw the Red Pagoda towering against the yellow sky.

P'eng looked back and through Hampton's goggles to the man's eyes. Something had changed there. The glance was clean and clear. Alive.

P'eng looked at the empty gunner's pit and the hard empty ring of the Lewis mounts. He shifted his gaze and saw that Hampton was holding a soiled, square package as though it contained diamonds.

"Liang?" asked P'eng.

Hampton looked down at the captain. For a long while he said nothing. Finally:

"He and your intelligence man fought them off so that I could get away."

Hampton considered that for a moment and changed it.

"No. They fought them off so that these dispatches would arrive."

"You . . . ?"

"I squared the account as good as I could." Hampton's voice rose in pitch and he looked angrily down at the officer. "Did you think I'd run without making them *pay?*"

A Chinese mechanic came up on the other side and stood there waiting. Hampton heard him and turned.

"Gas and oil," said Hampton. "And strain the gas!"

P'eng knew the story then. He watched Hampton climbing down.

"You are going up again?"

"As soon as I deliver these," said Hampton.

"You need a gunner?" said P'eng.

"Yes. And guns."

"I'll go."

Hampton stopped and turned. He saw the sling and the cane, the drawn face. But he saw more. Two dark eyes, alive and eager.

"Sorry," said Hampton. "You couldn't stand the knocking around. Tomorrow, next week . . ."

In sudden compassion, Hampton took the man's arm and helped him across the field to the gate.

Hampton delivered the dispatches as though they had been written on sheets of beaten gold in letters fashioned of precious stones.

Not with fanfare. He stepped around the colonel's desk, took the colonel's arm and laid the square package securely in the colonel's strong hand.

The elderly officer glanced up inquiringly. Hampton usually threw things on his desk in a careless, listless way. But now there was something in the intense care of the gesture, the studied soberness of Hampton's face, which made the colonel look back at the dispatches with a little awe.

Hampton stood where he was, beside the colonel's chair. He showed no signs of moving and looked as though he wanted to read the dispatches over the colonel's shoulder.

That, too, was unusual.

The colonel broke the seals by inserting his long fingernails under them. The movement made small, crisp pops which were loud in the stillness of the room.

Hampton could not read the characters but his gaze remained steadily upon the pages.

The colonel read them through, placed them carefully before him on his desk and stared at them with unfocused, thoughtful eyes.

The colonel's gaze went down through the sheets, through the clutter of paper under them. He saw a column of marching troops under the colors of Chiang. He saw a climbing stream of trucks lumbering around the curve of a hill, stretching out endlessly to the horizon. He saw the barrels of cannon under the covering canvas and the jostling boxes of shells.

He saw sections of pontoons aboard the slow, relentless trucks, heard them creaking under their lashings, saw them overlaid with the film of long travel.

The colonel's strong hands clutched the edge of a half-opened drawer. His gaze went down through the papers again, down to a pontoon bridge across the surging Yellow

River. Down to a column of hurrying troops surging over the rattling planks. Down to a thunderous barrage of covering artillery fire against which no troops could stand.

The colonel's eyes saw the Red Pagoda tumbling, shattered, into the city's deserted streets.

The colonel turned and looked up at Hampton.

"You know what is here?" said the Chinese, tapping his long fingernails against the reports.

"I think I do," said Hampton.

"Chiang is going to bridge the Yellow River. With the artillery he will have for covering fire, we can't hope to stop him. We haven't the guns, Hampton."

"No," said Hampton.

The colonel shook himself and got himself together. "We marched seven thousand miles to get to Shensi. We shall not be driven out now! Hampton. You have your plane ready?"

"Yes."

"Hampton. You will search out that convoy of trucks and hinder them in every way possible with machine-gun fire from the air."

Hampton looked strangely at the colonel. He looked up at the wall as though he could pierce it and see the Red Pagoda.

Hampton's answer came slowly.

"The Bristol is not in good condition. To operate fifty miles inside Chiang's territory would be fatal to both myself and the ship."

The colonel sat back in his chair, gaping. He put his feet on the floor and turned. Hampton backed up.

"At a time like this," said the colonel, "you speak of what cannot be done."

"I am sorry," said Hampton.

"You refuse to harass that convoy?"

"Yes," replied Hampton.

The colonel looked closely at the pilot. Disappointment gradually crept in upon the tragic face.

"You may go, Hampton."

Chapter Six

TENSION grew in the city as the days passed. False rumors blew up like whirlwinds to sweep down the streets and draw the people into excited, fearful groups.

Soldiers, scooping rice out of bowls with their chopsticks, would stop with the dish against their chin, sticks motionless, to stare straight ahead, listening. Nervously, then, they would go on.

Officers found occasion to visit the walls a dozen times a day to stand there looking out toward the Yellow River several miles away, drawn into silent pairs, listening and watching.

Hampton was seated on a bench on the sunny side of his quarters, looking up at the Red Pagoda, head back against the wall. But he was not relaxed. His face was hard and his eyes thoughtful.

Captain P'eng found him sitting there. P'eng limped around the corner of the red building and came slowly up to Hampton. P'eng looked up at the Red Pagoda and then slowly back to the pilot. He sank down wearily on the bench, drawing a small pattern in the dust which covered the pavement.

"It was not good to refuse," said P'eng.

Hampton had not glanced his way.

"The soldiers are muttering."

"Let them talk," said Hampton, looking straight ahead and up. "Do you think *I* care?"

"There is discussion of . . ." P'eng's cane made a circular pattern in the dust, attached a long line to it, fashioned an angular bar, without realizing that he had drawn a gibbet.

Hampton did not seem to hear. He appeared to be watching the sentry on the top of the tower—but he was not.

"You might have saved us," said P'eng.

Hampton heard that. He turned to the captain and his face grew tense.

"Saved you with the Bristol?" said Hampton. "With a ship that might come down any second? I know what I am doing, P'eng."

"You could have stacked up the convoy and given some of our far-flung troops a chance to arrive. We have no artillery."

"I might have cracked up," said Hampton. "And I might have been given the *coup de grâce*. What is the sense in that?"

"There is talk . . ." said P'eng, drawing another bar on his gibbet.

"Let them talk."

Hampton was once more looking up at the Red Pagoda.

At one o'clock that night, Hampton sat up in bed, staring into the thick gloom of his room. He was not yet wholly awake, and against the background of darkness his thoughts ran in a continuous, swift chain.

He had heard thunder.

It came again, a rumbling, crashing blast. Far away. The echoes rolled ominously through the walled town. Another crash of artillery jarred the red buildings.

Hampton crawled out of his bed and went to the door. A cold wind was blowing, eating through him. He looked at the inky sky.

Suddenly light flared like summer lightning, throwing the Red Pagoda into smoky silhouette. Darkness again. Light again. This time more guns had opened up. The sweeping curves of the tall tower were sharp against the yellow flashes.

The shivering explosions were like physical blows against the town. Soldiers were running, rifles were clanking. Calls were thin, beaten down by the bombardment.

Lightning flashed again to the east and showed up an entire company sprinting for the gate. They dashed around the base of the pagoda and vanished from sight.

The wind was cold.

Hampton dropped the curtain which was his door and went back to his bed. He crawled in between the cold blankets, the thunder torturing his ears.

"Let them talk," he muttered.

It was hard to tell when dawn really came. The east had been alight for hours, more and more as battery after battery of artillery had been swung into Chiang's line.

But dawn was there and the sun was a round ball, so dim a man could look straight at it without hurting his eyes.

Hampton stepped outside his door. The wind rumpled his hair and made the edges of his jacket flap against him.

He looked down the deserted street and saw P'eng hobbling toward the gate, buckling on a revolver belt as he went.

P'eng saw Hampton but it was only a passing glance. P'eng did not stop.

Hampton walked down across the pavement, the wind hurling up small flurries of dust to meet him. Hampton did not notice that it was cold.

He entered a small hut which was fitted out for cooking. One lone Chinese was there nervously stirring a bubbling caldron of rice. He looked up when Hampton came near, saw who it was and looked down into the pot.

"Give me a cup of tea," said Hampton.

The Chinese did not turn.

Hampton went to the cupboard and took down a caddy. He dumped some leaves into a dixie and poured some hot water on them. The steam curled up and lay damply against his cheeks, cold the next instant.

He reached back to the shelf and ferreted out a bottle of rice wine. He pulled the cork with his teeth and emptied half a tumblerful into the dixie.

Taking the hot concoction with him he went back to the door and stood there looking out, looking up. The sun was directly behind the Red Pagoda, giving it a luminous fringe around each cupola.

Hampton sipped his tea.

He came back after a little and set the empty dixie on a bench. The Chinese kept on stirring the pot of rice he knew no one would ever eat.

Walking leisurely, Hampton went out. He crossed the pavement to his hut, stepped in and looked around. He had a few trinkets which connected him with a remote and half-forgotten past. A picture of himself as an Army cadet. A picture of a girl whose name he no longer remembered. A pair of spurs with silver bolívars for rowels. A pair of silver-handled brushes with most of the bristles missing.

He strewed them out on the table and looked at them. His face did not change. He swept them back into his kit and dropped the whole into a bin full of empty bottles and stained papers by the door.

He took his helmet from a peg on the wall and put it on, looking at himself in a cracked mirror. He was very careful with the helmet, taking some time to adjust it exactly right. He dropped his hands from it and looked at himself for a long while. Then he turned toward the door.

He crossed the pavement again, but this time he headed for the gate, skirting the foot of the Red Pagoda. He looked at it as he passed, looked up at the high top. No sentry was there now. The tower was empty.

Hampton went on through the gate, listening to the growing crackle of rifle fire which made a hysterical clatter above the lowering thunder of the cannonade.

At the hangar he found no mechanics. The Bristol was silently spreading its tattered wings in the gloom. It had flown too many hours, had seen too much of the world. It had dodged too many bullets and seen too many men die.

A dolly was under the tail. Hampton took the handle and

began to pull. The Bristol eased tail first out of the crude hangar and began to tremble when the cold wind whistled in the wings.

Hampton pulled it farther and then, working slowly and methodically, turned it around and into the brisk blast.

He chocked the wheels and turned on his ignition. He pulled the prop through and it caught. Slowly he went back to the pit and cut the throttle to idling.

He had to let it warm, but then he was in no hurry. The thunder of artillery was louder here. The canvas hangar door was trembling under the concussion. The clatter of rifle fire grew higher.

Hampton sat down on an empty oil tin and pulled out a package of cigarettes. There was just one left. He put it in between his lips and felt it stick because of the dry cold. He reached into another pocket and found just one match. He lighted it and pulled smoke into his lungs.

Looking down he saw he still held the empty package and the burned match. He read the label and then, with slow, nerveless fingers, crumpled it up and threw it away.

He looked at the match and seemed to find something interesting in the blackened, dead stump. Something like a smile twitched at the corner of his mouth.

He threw the match away.

The Bristol was warm. The Rolls was clanking its worn bearings, spewing out smoke from the stack. The wind whisked the smoke away into nothingness.

Hampton ground the cigarette stub under his heel and

looked down at it. The frayed white paper stirred a little in the slipstream and then lay still.

Hampton went back into the hangar. He backed out in a moment, hauling a case of ten-kilo bombs after him. He broke the lid open and began to hand them, one by one, into the rear cockpit, making sure they were all live.

He shoved the empty case out of his way and pulled his own chocks. The Bristol trundled ahead, but without haste Hampton thrust his boot in the stirrup and went over the side.

Chapter Seven

THE panorama of battle unfolded itself as he built altitude. Far to the south everything was calm. The Red Pagoda still stood above the city walls, a finger pointing straight up toward the murky sky.

To the east the plains were alive with men in gray uniforms—Chiang's men, coming into a vortex at the pontoon bridge. Laid out in even rows behind earthworks were batteries of artillery, snouts jabbing and recoiling and roaring. Chiang had done his work well.

The pontoon bridge was a black line drawn perpendicularly across the Yellow River. It seemed to be alive, its surface flowing toward the western shore.

On the western side, shells were hitting, sending up geysers of gray and white smoke, gouging into earthworks, caving in trenches, blotting out riflemen.

The bridge continued to flow. Regiment after regiment was moving across. Division after division was waiting to start. Here and there on the planking a man had dropped. Now and then an officer broke ranks to dump an obstructing body into the stream.

The CPVAJR Army lay against their sandbags, carefully conserving their bullets, shooting to kill, shooting until they were killed.

The first line had been crumpled back. Several thousand of Chiang's troops had made the crossing. In waves they threw themselves against the earthworks and trenches.

Bayonets flashed in the smoky light. Gray dots were strewn on the yellow shore.

The artillery was pummeling the second line of defense, having marched with shrapnel boots over the first.

Systematic, deadly, bound to succeed.

Crumple up a line, take it with waves, hold it. Crumple up the next line, take it with waves, hold it.

Feed shells into the rebels!

Feed men over the bridge!

The efficient machine strode forward and on.

Hampton was high. No one was watching him. No one had even heard him above the deafening din.

He looked down at the problem below. It was all laid out for him on a corpse-strewn chessboard. In miniature. Unreal. But Hampton knew that men were dying. He watched them stumble and fall. He watched them surge up out of trenches in suicidal attempts to stop Chiang's machine. He saw them go down, swallowed by smoke and shrapnel and a gray blanket of charging men.

Hampton looked at the bridge.

At least a third of Chiang's forces were across. The other two thirds were waiting. At the moment, man for man, Chiang's forces on the western bank were outnumbered two to one. Without the artillery, the fighting troops would be helpless, engulfed, hacked down by the valiant CPVAJR Army.

Without the bridge, Chiang would lose.

Only one bridge.

No timber within several hundred miles.

Without a third of his troops, Chiang would have to withdraw, leaving the CPVAJR Army in possession of thousands of rifles, hundreds of thousands of rounds of captured ammunition.

Hampton turned and looked back at the city.

The Red Pagoda was a tall, pointing finger at the sky.

Hampton flew down the river a few miles and banked around to come back. The Rolls sounded bad. It would not last very long. It would not have to last.

Hampton looked down at the bridge which seemed to flow. The planking was spread with a moving gray blanket.

Hampton put the Bristol's nose down into a steep dive and looked over his cowl, through his prop, at the pontoon bridge.

The Rolls began to wind up.

The tach came over and around and stuck.

The ASI went up, up, up—until it, too, could go no farther.

The pontoon bridge began to get big through the spinning prop. Suddenly it turned a lighter color and stopped flowing. Men were looking up.

They saw a streaking plane above them, doubling, trebling in size. They heard the torturing yowl of the engine even above the thunder of their guns.

They looked back toward the eastern shore. They jammed in the center, some trying to go on, some trying to go back. Officers beat about them with the flat of their swords, screaming unheard into the mounting din.

In the CPVAJRA trenches, men saw the plane and stopped firing, rolling halfway off their guns to stare, open-mouthed, at the streaking javelin.

The attacking troops heard it and wheeled, stopping motionless to stare upward and back at the bridge.

The artillerymen behind Chiang's guns forgot to yank their lanyards.

The only sound in all the world was the rising crescendo of a worn-out Rolls-Royce engine.

The men on the bridge ceased to move. They looked straight up at the bright disc of the prop which was coming at them faster than their eyes could focus upon it.

Again they surged toward the east, toward the west, only to remain where they were.

A man stood up on the western ramparts. He dropped his smoking pistol to his side and leaned heavily upon his cane.

The world was so still and yet so filled with the grinding, shrieking of wings and engine.

Hampton could see eyes in the faces now. He could see buttons and insignia.

He glanced back toward the ten-kilo bombs which rattled in his gunner's pit. He turned and faced the bridge. One hand ripped open his safety belt and then returned to the throttle as though it needed to be held full on.

He saw all the bridge, then the center half, then the center alone.

The Bristol hit!

The bombs in the rear pit exploded in the same instant.

STORIES from the GOLDEN AGE

☐ Yes, I would like to receive my **FREE CATALOG** featuring all 80 volumes of the *Stories from the Golden Age Collection and more!*

Name

Shipping Address

City   State   ZIP

Telephone   E-mail

Check other genres you are interested in: ☐ SciFi/Fantasy ☐ Western ☐ Mystery

FREE SHIPPING!
NO PURCHASE REQUIRED

6 Books • 8 Stories
Illustrations • Glossaries

6 Audiobooks • 12 CDs
8 Stories • Full color 40-page booklet

Fold on line and tape

IF YOU ENJOYED READING THIS BOOK, GET THE ACTION/ADVENTURE COLLECTION **AND** SAVE 25%

BOOK SET
~~$59.50~~ $45.00
ISBN: 978-1-61986-089-6

AUDIOBOOK SET
~~$77.50~~ $58.00
ISBN: 978-1-61986-090-2

☐ Check here if shipping address is same as billing.

Name

Billing Address

City   State   ZIP

Telephone   E-mail

Credit/Debit Card #: _____

Card ID # (last 3 or 4 digits): _____

Exp Date: _____/_____ Date (month/day/year): _____/_____/_____

Order Total *(CA and FL residents add sales tax)*: _____

To order online, go to: **www.GoldenAgeStories.com** or call toll-free **1-877-8GALAXY** or 1-323-466-7815

Something was thrown from the front pit, far out into the middle of the Yellow River.

The pontoons caved under the shock, disappeared completely under the terrific explosion. Flames rocketed up against the sullen sky, brightening it for an instant.

Fragments of wood, bits of guns, chunks of men, began to patter back into the turgid stream.

Only one pontoon remained solidly against the shore. The others were gone. The river was flowing free.

The whole world, then, was still. Men had not yet recovered from the shock.

Only one man moved.

P'eng stood on the western ramparts, smoking pistol at his side. He dropped it to the dusty earth and slowly raised his grimy hand to his tattered cap and held it there in salute.

The depths of the Yellow River gave up a shadowy thing. It came to the surface and turned slowly over. Its face was ripped apart. The water around it was streaked with faint red streamers as it was borne downstream.

It turned.

Far away against the sky was the tall, graceful finger of the Red Pagoda, pointing at the sky.

Water was closing over Hampton for the last time as he saw it. He tried to smile as he went down. He tried to say the words:

"That guy was right."

The Crate Killer

The Crate Killer

H E knew the ship would come apart. He knew these frail but shapely wings could never stand nine Gs. He knew the earth, eighteen thousand feet below, might or might not feel again the footsteps of Jumper Bailey.

But that was his job. If the wings were in danger of pulling off, then Jumper Bailey would leave them fluttering somewhere far behind while the bomb which would be the fuselage would keep on going down.

That was his job, test pilot, and that was his ultimate end—a crash.

He circled in the blue, looking down at the mammoth checkerboard of earth, at the doll-size hangars and barracks. A white line was a river, a thin streak was a road. Those regular dots were an orchard.

He listened to his engine and found the sweet song good. He looked through his glass hood at the yellow wings and had misgivings as to their strength. Too bad this pleasant craft would soon explode all over the sky.

He was eight times a caterpillar, was Bailey. Eight times he had hit the silk—much to the sly amusement of his brother lieutenants. A cat, they said, had nine lives and this last one had better be conserved. He bore their jibes as well as he could,

He knew the earth, eighteen thousand feet below,
might or might not feel again the footsteps
of Jumper Bailey.

knowing he was not nearly as responsible for hitting the silk as he seemed. Jumper, they called him, and rightly.

During the airmail scramble he had pulled twice on his rip cord. Before that, two incidents had caused him to abandon his ship in the sky via the parachute route. The powers that be had long ago decided that the best way of utilizing Bailey's unique aptitude for bailing out would be to make a test pilot out of him.

The injustice of it weighed upon him. The last four leaps had been from ships which no longer possessed their wings, and what pilot ever rode after the fins were gone?

Because of that very reputation, the ships he was given to test were never the good, reliable crates. He always got the questionable planes like this new, untried attack.

Habitually he looked to his ring and found it to be where it was supposed to be. His harness was in place and he was sitting on the pack.

Eighteen thousand feet below, his superiors were getting stiff necks trying to catch the flash of sun on his wings and Jumper Bailey delayed no longer.

With a wistful sigh for the dear dead days, he hauled back into a mushy stall.

Tail pointing at the ground and nose at the sky, the attack hung for an instant like a model from the ceiling.

Abruptly it whipstalled.

Light as a handkerchief in the pit, Bailey nudged the rudders and slammed the gun all the way up the trident.

With a startled yowl the engine shot the tach all the way around the dial.

The earth tipped up until the rivers threatened to spill out of their beds.

Straight down, wide open, the attack plane streaked toward destruction.

The earth was a soup plate, then a funnel. Trees and fields flowed uphill toward the rim. The hangars were sucked down into the vortex.

Up came the ASI, quivering to reach three hundred. The merciless pilot kept the screaming motor at full gun.

The altimeter began to drop. Eighteen, seventeen, sixteen . . .

Shrieking wings and thundering engine made a gigantic discord of tortured sound which shook the windows of the world and shivered the eardrums into deafness.

Down, down, down. Fifteen, fourteen, thirteen . . .

The compass floated rockily, white numbers out of sight. The fire extinguisher came half out of its bracket and floated there, thumbing its nose at Newton.

Held up against his belt by the terrific force of acceleration, Bailey was glad to have something solid to hold his stomach in place.

The ASI came up to terminal velocity. The ship could dive no faster. The wall of air was equal at last to the drive of the roaring engine.

Bailey eased the throttle a notch. He glanced at the array of meters which the engineers would read later on. A smoky plate showed a vertical line which, when the pullout came, would show the angle. Another meter read in gravities and Bailey knew he would have to pull the needle up to nine.

He'd do it, even if she wouldn't stay together.

The hangars were doubling, trebling in size. Men could be seen now. Men in uniforms, men in slacks. The khaki top of the crash wagon caught Bailey's eye. It'd better be ready.

Twelve, eleven, ten thousand feet . . .

His head felt terrible, his ears were hotbeds of lightning. But with stick and careful feet he held the attack in its groove. A caterpillar only had nine lives, they said. He'd better be careful of this one. The hood over his head was all ready to slide back and let him out. Now if the wings floated clear and didn't pin him down . . .

Eight thousand . . . seven . . .

Telegraph poles along the highway were beginning to lean out away from him. Trees bent. The funnel of green and yellow and dun was flowing uphill away from the field.

He was the bomb and there was the target.

The ship sounded like ten million cats in a fight. Shaking and shuddering as though scared, as though knowing its immediate fate, the attack lanced down and ever down.

The pullout was at hand.

He came back on the stick. The flippers fought him. He hauled harder. The flippers bit.

Both hands on the grip, teeth set with effort but ready to open and yell, Bailey yanked the attack horizontal.

Like a deflected arrow, still shrieking, the plane, for an instant, tried to hold its wings.

An inverted pile driver hit the belly. Bailey's yell was cut off in midflight. The blood was out of his head, he was almost unconscious, but he felt the terrific force of the jolt.

He saw the wings soar outward in a cloud of yellow chunks, sailing upward and backward. . . .

The fuselage lurched. Engine still on, the stripped hull raced downward again.

Bailey fought through fogs of blackness and parted the red curtains before his eyes. Things started to turn green again. He could see white faces straight ahead—which was straight down. He could see the crash wagon driver leaping for his seat. He could see men scattering. . . .

Bailey unsnapped his belt. He had a thousand feet and that was little enough.

He thrust backwards on his hood. Air crashed into his hot face. He pried himself off the seat. The slipstream caught his chest and almost broke his spine over the turtleback.

He could see the grass, blade by blade. Everything was running back from him. The earth was more a cone than ever and he was going to plow straight on through the vortex clear to China.

He forced himself up an inch at a time. It was hard work. The air was like a stream of bricks against him.

The fuselage turned over. Bailey gave a kick.

Tumbling like a ricocheting bullet, he bowled through the blue.

He had no time to look for the ship. The earth was right there beside him.

He snatched the ring. Silk cracked as the pilot chute streaked out. The grass was just under his boots and he was going to hit it ten times faster than an express train.

Jumper Bailey

Abruptly his harness yanked at his legs, spinning him, almost tearing him limb from limb.

He sailed out in a wide arc and came swinging back down as though on a trapeze. Earth slammed against his shoulders and the chute laid over, trying to get away from him, towing him along the field.

Rolling stiffly over, he seized the shrouds and spilled out the unwanted wind.

Bailey sat down on the crumpled canopy and fished out a cigarette. His hands were shaking, of course, but he was no whiter than a freshly laundered shirt.

He lit up and took a drag. A siren was yowling and men were yelling and boots were raising dust.

"You all right, sir?" cried a sergeant, much more excited than Bailey.

"Okay," said Jumper, exhaling blue smoke.

He had not heard the plane hit. He had been too busy listening for his personal crash. But he saw the cloud of black and greasy fumes and he knew that the crate was burning.

They took the chute harness off him and he scaled to the seat of the crash wagon, cautioning the driver to go slow.

He did not immediately report because that, he thought, was rather silly. On the way down he had made some notes, he thought, but he could not now remember a single line of them.

Stiffly he climbed down and entered a small building. Several brother lieutenants opened the way for him, silently regarding him.

Bailey pulled off his suit and threw it on a bench. He turned to the mirror and for several seconds stared at his somewhat smudged face.

Finally Donovan said, "Nine lives, Jumper."

"That's the last one, isn't it?" said Bailey with an apologetic smile.

He noted that not one of them asked after his health, which would be a natural and polite question. No man ever rose to high places in the army by repeatedly hitting his silk. It might be a tragedy for another man to come that close to being killed, but where Jumper Bailey was involved . . . well, there was a limit to all things. Consensus said that all Bailey had to do was look at a ship and it would come apart in the air. No squadron would have taken him into its complement because, though airmen are *never* superstitious, still you couldn't be too careful about a jinx.

When the commercial test pilot had tried that attack, it had stayed together. But with Bailey in the pit . . .

He put on his cap and straightened his blouse and went

out to report. The attack was still burning in a circle of wing fragments.

Three civilians were standing glumly beside a railing. They stared at him and then one of them whispered, without knowing that Bailey could hear, "Damn it, it's just our luck. He's a hoodoo, they tell me. Bails out on the slightest provocation. Never been known to stick to a ship. . . . "

Bailey cringed a little and went on, trying to pretend he had not heard.

Things had quieted down considerably. Three pilots were heading for the hangar to take off for nerve tonic after the crash. The major was seen to enter his office and Bailey, at some distance, followed him.

He passed the orderly in the outer office, seeing that Major Harvey was sitting down at his desk. Harvey was not exactly pleased.

Two things had happened that morning which had not been calculated to sweeten the major's temper. An inspecting colonel had discovered that two trucks bore no insignia whatever and he had upbraided the major about it. And the major's wife had inadvisedly showed him a charge account bill she had accidentally run to three figures.

Furthermore, this particular attack ship had been built partly due to specifications for attack ships the major had laid down and it was, in effect, a brainchild.

"Come in, Lieutenant," said the major, sweetly. "Come in and sit down. I trust you are not injured."

"No, sir, I'm okay."

"Now just what was the trouble?"

Bailey had been in Miami once when a hurricane had arrived. Just before its coming the atmosphere had been very still.

"I . . . I pulled out and . . . the wings came off."

"Yes, yes to be sure. The wings came off. Now just when did they start to come off?"

"I came out of it and leveled off and bingo, there they went."

"I suppose," said the major, dripping molasses, "that you couldn't have noticed anything else. You were probably busy pushing back the hood, getting ready to jump."

"No, sir. I—"

"And isn't it possible that you were so occupied in locating your rip cord that you allowed her to go past nine Gs? I mean to say, Bailey—"

"No, sir. She was clean out of it when she decided to go. . . ."

"Lieutenant, just why you were wished off on us as a test pilot, I don't know. I believe this is the ninth time you have left your ship, is it not?"

"Well, yes, sir, I—"

"The first time, I believe it was, you got caught in the fog over the mountains and you bailed out."

"Yes, sir. I was out of gas and—"

"And when we went to look for the wreckage, we discovered that you were not over the mountains at all and that your ship had practically flown itself in, breaking only the landing gear."

"Yes, sir, I—"

"I do not think there is any need rehashing the other fiascos.

You probably have heard, by this time, that the United States Army has to pay out good money for planes and that we hire good pilots to fly those planes, not to break them up. Do I make myself clear?"

"Yes, sir."

"This afternoon," continued the relentless major, "I was closely observing your flight. If you had brought the ship out smoothly as it should have been, there would have been no accident. But you jerked the plane into a horizontal line of flight and pulled her apart. It's a wonder you weren't crushed in the pit, more's the pity."

"It came out hard," protested Bailey.

"I thought so. It happens, Lieutenant, that you are assigned to this field to test newly engineered planes. There is unhappily no other pilot here assigned to this duty. But there is one more attack which will have to be tested. To give you the benefit of the doubt, we will see that the wings are considerably strengthened. As soon as this is done, you will test the ship. I might mention that this is probably the last ship you will ever test because, as soon as I can replace you, I will ask for your resignation. Do I make myself clear?"

"Y-Yes, sir."

"You are very bad for the morale here, Lieutenant, and this is the only thing I can do. Very good, then. Hold yourself in readiness for another test next week—and make sure you don't muff it—your last."

"Yes, sir," said Bailey, miserably withdrawing.

Another man might have grown sullen and abusive under the apparently unfair charge, but not Jumper Bailey. He had fought his way up through the ranks to his wings and bars and they meant a great deal to him, but more than that, he respected the mandates of higher authority, considering them unalterable.

He knew definitely that he himself was at fault. He knew that the pilot is the captain of his craft and that the ship must not be deserted until the grate of the Reaper's scythe could be heard above the motor's dying cough.

He knew that he was referred to as the "ace" wherever he went because he had brought down more than five planes, each one the property of the United States.

Often he had heard it said of him that it was about time he turned into a butterfly, he had been a caterpillar so often.

He knew he had cost his government something like a million dollars while he himself was worth, according to his insurance policy, only ten thousand.

He did not blame his brethren for steering wide of him because he knew that while there is *never* such a thing as a jinx, a pilot can never be too careful.

He realized that a test pilot must, from time to time, bail out to save his neck, but he realized also that test pilots, being considered as good as dead men anyway, are rarely accorded either glory or sympathy until they are turned under the sod.

For ten days Jumper Bailey kept to himself, sitting for hours in the dark corners of bars drinking exactly nine drinks per diem.

There was a fascination about the number nine. That many times a caterpillar and the tenth coming up.

But while he waited for the strengthening of the new attack's wings, events were in the making at the field.

The orderly sergeant had heard the major's ultimatum to Bailey and the orderly sergeant, after the custom longstanding in all armies everywhere, imparted the news to his mess. These sergeants mentioned something of it to their wives and, via grapevine, it gradually came to the ears of Mrs. Harvey who, still feeling ruffled over her curtailed accounts, barked it at the major.

"It's all very well," said Mrs. Harvey to Major Harvey, "for you to tell me that you sweat your life's blood for this puny pay. You work hard, I don't think. You sit at a desk passing out orders and playing the tyrant to your men just like you do to me!"

"What do you mean by that?" barked the major.

"It's all over the post what you're going to do to that poor Lieutenant Bailey. Talk all you want about his being a jinx, but for all your fine orders, nobody ever saw *you* risking your fat neck."

The damage was done. The words said for spite rankled long in the major's breast.

He would sit at his desk mulling it wrathfully. So it was all over the post, was it? So he was yellow, was he? So he sent men to do jobs he wouldn't do, did he? Damn that Bailey. A lady's man, that's what. Test pilot be damned. What was it that a test pilot had nobody else had?

And the final upshot of this mental shelling was that the major stood on the line in full flying kit the morning the new attack was to be tested.

Fearing the fellow had gone crazy, the mechanics and greaseballs walked softly as they rolled out the ship.

Bailey appeared, looking wistful and rolling the number nine around inside his head. He saw the major, stopped and gaped.

"You . . . you going up this morning, sir?"

"You'll see whether I'll go up or not!"

"But, sir, this is my job."

"Don't tell me what your job is. This ship can be tested with her gunner aboard. Get in the rear pit!"

"But . . . I mean . . . Yes, sir."

Bailey, with many misgivings, knew he was about to be shown how to test a plane. On the other occasion he had ridden with a sandbag in the gunner's pit and now he was to be the sandbag himself.

A captain or two tried to argue the major out of it, but Harvey was somewhat set in his ways. They doubted his courage, he thought, when as a matter of fact nobody had been thinking anything of the kind.

The major glowered at Bailey, climbed in and slammed the hood in place. Bailey looked down between his knees and thankfully observed a stick connected there.

The major was a good pilot, of course, fond of his prowess and the marksmanship which was attested by the camera guns, vain about his reputation.

Bailey could not help seeing if his ring was in place, ready to rip. Guiltily he withdrew his hand from it.

The ship took off with a rush, nosed steeply up and began to scramble for altitude. The civilian observers down below grew rapidly smaller.

The engine was running like a sewing machine, the strengthened wings knifed the crisp air. All was well.

The windsock vanished, the world spread out to hazy horizons, the spider-webbing of highways stretched out to catch the fly which was the attack's shadow.

The big colored relief map of the world rolled out for Bailey's inspection. He folded his hands and tried to enjoy it but he was jumpy, missing the control of the ship, startled every time they struck a bump.

The air became smoother as they went up. And then it was cold and the earth was lost in a haze of unreality.

Three miles and more in the air, the major leveled out and cruised a short ways, getting back over the field. He turned and glared pugnaciously at Bailey as much as to say "I'll show you!"

Then, with attention to the business at hand, the major went over the hump, full gun and down.

Unprepared, Bailey had all the sickening sensation of going over the dips in a roller coaster. Amazed, he stared straight ahead, over the major's hood, over the engine, through the prop and at the earth.

For the first time he was a passenger on one of these rushing dives and he did not much care for it. Without the controls to think about, his mind was free to play with the multitude of lethal possibilities.

Gripping the cowl like a lady on her first hop, mouth open and eyes bulging, Bailey watched the earth hollow out, watched the hills sweep back, watched the rivers spread themselves and ripple.

His ears began to hurt and he yelled a little to make them stop. The engine was turning up, faster and faster, jangling in a bellow of protest. The wings squealed in shrill terror. Balled together, the ear-splitting screech of their descent thundered through the sky.

The major knew what he was doing. He slacked off when they reached terminal velocity and rode his streaking bomb like a cowboy sticks a plunging bronc.

Straight down. Wailing and yowling and braying at the tiny square which was the field far below. The cannonballs of old never traveled this fast. A freely falling body would have been left thousands of feet above them.

Nothing could stand the racking torture of that speed. Nothing made of fabric and metal could stand the pullout.

Nine Gs it would have to be. Nine times the weight of the plane would slam the underside of those wings when the stick came back.

The major's two hundred pounds of muscle and bone would suddenly become eighteen hundred pounds. And if he came out too fast, moaned Bailey, the two of them would be mangled to lifeless rags by the invisible but inexorable weight of gravity.

And even if they lived through that, the wings might come

off as they had before and send them plunging straight down without control, faster than a bomb was ever dropped.

Bailey felt for his rip cord again and drew his hand away. He felt for the snap of his belt as though to make sure he could part it in an instant and hated himself for doing it.

Down, down, down, to the tune of a siren's rave. Down like a hurled javelin at the blurring green and khaki of the world.

Bailey, holding hard, thought he smelled something. He sniffed again. Surely that couldn't be gasoline!

A fine spray was streaking back from the underside of the left wing, like a veil whipping there. Bailey's eyes grew round and scared, staring at it.

The vibration had parted the gas lines and the fluid was dousing the cowl, the fuselage. . . .

Bailey screamed into the tube, "We're soaked in gas!"

It was impossible to hear anything above the battering wail of the dive.

But the major saw it. His head turned to the left and stayed there an instant.

The fumes were thick and suffocating.

Six thousand feet up, not yet time for the pullout. But the major pulled.

The terrific force of gravity snatched the blood from Bailey's head. From force of habit he yelled loud and long to ease the tension of his bursting drums.

Almost unconscious as he was, he sat stiffly awaiting the crack and bang which would tell of the departure of the wings. But the jolt did not come.

They were racing even with the horizon again, all in one piece. The earth was still a long, long way off. The hangars were the size of pillboxes against the green.

The major hastily cut the mags but he was too late.

A puff of blue flame rolled up like a bowling ball over the cowl, burst and streaked savagely back at the hoods.

The attack went over into a slip and for an instant the black smoke rolled clear.

The engine was silent but the wings were shrill.

"Jump!" roared the major.

Paralyzed, Bailey sat where he was.

Harvey stood up in the buffeting blast, face scorched, collar smoking. "Jump, damn you!"

Bailey seemed to be in a trance.

The major fought to get Bailey's hood open from the outside and then suddenly gave it up. With a despairing look and with one last, pleading shout, seeing that Bailey was evidently incapable of saving himself, the major went over the side.

Harvey instantly shrank to the size of a walnut against the green. White silk bellied over him, hiding him.

The roar of flames resounded in Bailey's ears.

He had kicked the tail out of the major's way.

The left wing was a cloud of black streamers interspersed with wicked green tongues. The searing heat pounded against Bailey's hood.

The wing would be burned through in an instant.

Bailey shifted the stick and kicked right rudder, putting the left wing down and slipping in that direction.

The furnace blast was swept across the cowl again for a roaring instant and then the right wing took the brunt, leaving its mate to smolder in a tatter of fabric.

The all-metal fuselage, soaked inside and out, began to warp in the heat.

Bailey pumped at his extinguisher and flew with his knees, dousing his firewall. His boots were ovens, cooking his feet. In spite of the fumes he could smell his own hair burning.

He turned the foaming fluid on himself and held the attack in its giddy, swooping slip.

He brought down the tail and almost made the plane fly sideways.

The whistle of the wings blended with the hiss of the flames. He could not see how badly off were his wings. They might drop from him any instant.

Baked, broiled, seared and fried, Bailey cocked a calculating if singed eye upon the runway. He went into a steeper skid. He let down the wheels with an auxiliary crank.

The smoke was so dense before him that he could but dimly see the buildings ahead. He slammed the ship down to earth. It bounced perilously and crunched down again.

With his rudder he directed the blackly geysering nose at the squat firehouse.

Bricks raised up before him and he stamped his heels on the brakes.

A man in asbestos grabbed him and yanked him out of the pit. Chemical extinguishers sang louder than the flames.

They laid Bailey out on the grass. He was gummy with pyrene and black as charcoal. His boots were cracked and smoking. But his suit and helmet and gloves had spared most of him from the flames and he was not burned but only heated through.

Presently a being who trailed a wad of parachute silk dragged dolefully up to the now smoldering and surprisingly uninjured ship.

"Is he all right?" whispered Harvey.

Bailey, slightly knocked out and very dizzy, rose up on his elbows and peered from under blackened lashes at the major.

Bailey's voice was jubilant, like that of a man who has just received a pardon ten steps from the chair.

"I brought her down! I brought her down, I tell you! And I didn't touch my ring once. Not once, do you hear?"

Wings Over Ethiopia

Wings Over Ethiopia

FROM out the sandy waste came puffs of oily smoke, appearing magically against the tan of parched earth.

Larry Colter eased his left rudder and looked anxiously down at the twisting heat waves which sent the world crawling in wretched supplication to the mighty blast of the sun.

The engine of the Waco roared steadily on, deafening the men behind the puffs and the man in the rear cockpit who swung out crazily, holding hard to his slipstream-buffeted DeVry movie camera.

Larry Colter looked back to see if Bill Singer had noticed, but Bill Singer was intent upon getting his aerial action pictures of the Ethiopian War.

The puffs grew in volume. A flying wire parted with a vicious twang and then rippled back in the breeze, saber-slashing the wing fabric. Colter hauled hard on the stick and sent the laboring ship vaulting upstairs.

Good God, they were shooting at him!

Were they blind? What did those natives think this was?

Bill Singer clutched his precious camera and glared, pointing determinedly down. Colter shook his head and pointed at the flying wire. Singer stared blankly at it, seeing it for the first time, and then, remembering why they were there, he pointed down again.

Colter sighed and eased the stick ahead. He did not like this job. Those blacks were under the delusion that every and any ship was an Italian bomber, ready to sock them into heaven with one wallop.

The puffs swelled out again. Black powder, guessed Colter. He felt a jar run through the ship, then another. At five hundred feet, a machine gun stood a chance.

And then the motor quit cold and the wires whistled shrilly and the heat waves batted them about like a squirrel in a cage. Bill Singer was still grinding out film.

Colter picked out a spot on the flat plain and knew that the worst would happen. He had been driven half-crazy with the hunch for a day and a half.

But money was money when it ran into five grand and Colter had been very much on the ground and on the beach. He had taken part in the late Greek Rebellion, a flyer's part, and had gotten away with his life, but little cash. He had flown his ship to Asmara before his cash and gas gave out and then, after many months, this war had started and had found him irresolute as to which side to take.

And then Bill Singer of World Newsreel had come along with an offer. Bill Singer had wanted fighting pictures from the air and he had gotten them. It had all looked so simple. Just buzz over the line to Adwa and perhaps a little further, get some pictures of the fighting from a safe distance and then return. Yes, they had the pictures, but by the looks of that ragged mob jumping out of the trench over to the right, the pictures would never be developed.

Bill Singer had permission from the Italian High Command. The High Command, with a little palm grease, had said certainly. It was dangerous, and if the United States wouldn't hold them responsible in case of death . . . Papers to sign, permission granted.

The lower they sank, the hotter it became. The thermometer must be jumping around a hundred and fifty degrees. Heat lift slammed them and dropped them and slapped them off their course. Larry Colter, hard-boiled veteran of many such fights, fought the stick and felt for the ground.

"What's the matter?" cried Singer through the hissing quiet.

"Gas line, oil line, I dunno," replied Colter, not looking back.

"You think they'll treat us okay?"

"I dunno," said Colter.

They hit and bounced and floated and hit again. They narrowly missed a deep wash, ground looped and skidded to a dusty stop.

"You speak Amharic?" said Colter.

"What's that?"

"That's their language. I don't."

81

Bill Singer, thin-faced and quick of movement, stabbed his pale glance at the oncoming horde of rifle-waving Ethiopians. Then his profession got the better of his anxiety. He propped up the DeVry on the cowl and began to crank with just the proper speed.

The white-robed men slowed up and approached warily. They were big fellows, their woolly heads bared to the sizzling sun. They wore, for the most part, white cotton trousers and a split-sided long white coat which was tightly girded by a very wide bandolier bristling with glittery shells.

A man in the lead wearing a lion's tail stopped, held his rifle in a threatening position and yelled something which sounded like a cross between a seal's bark and a tiger's snarl.

"Quit it," said Colter to the cameraman. "They may think you're trying to shoot them." Colter stood up in the cockpit. He was very tall and lean and his face was hard-bitten and his eyes were light blue like a Syrian cat's.

The soldiers cautiously surrounded the plane, pointing at it, talking excitedly, patting their Lebels, Mannlichers and Sniders and generally congratulating themselves.

Colter looked them over. This, he knew, was a bad spot. He glanced about for an officer.

Finally, a rather handsome black, dressed in khaki and bearing a button like a target in his cap, stepped out with drawn automatic and motioned for Colter to step down.

Singer began to grind at his camera again and the natives scowled. Singer stopped and wiped the perspiration from his shining face.

"You speak English?" said Colter to the officer.

The man shook his head and answered in Amharic. Colter nodded in the negative and then, with a deep sigh, decided that he would have to try Italian, of all things.

"*Parlate Italiano?*" said Colter.

"*Si, si! Io sono Dejazwach,*" replied the officer.

"Fine," said Colter, "then you'll have to help me out of here. I need a gas line, understand? *Datemi un tubo per la benzina.*"

"*No! No!*" cried the officer. "You do not understand, either that or you are mad. You are my prisoner of war. My men have shot you down, do you see? And now you are my prisoner. I must confiscate your airplane."

Colter shrugged. He had been afraid of that. He stepped closer to the officer and pulled some papers out of his pocket.

"You are the one who does not understand, *Capitano*. I am an American. The United States of America. I am not an Italian. This man here is a cameraman, see? *Un fotografo.* We came here to get pictures of your soldiers. Moving pictures. We are not Italian fliers. See, there are no guns on our ship."

The officer, Dejazwach, looked puzzled. The soldiers about him, who understood not a word of what was being said, pressed close to them. Singer got out of the plane and came up.

The sun broiled them and the heat waves danced and the argument became lengthy. Colter began to get angry.

Suddenly a thin, booming sound came out of the north, growing in volume with every passing second.

The Ethiopians turned and stared into the sky. They moved nervously, glancing back at their officer. Abruptly, they broke and dived for the trench.

The officer looked at the plane and the two Americans,

fidgeting with his hands. He was not quite certain what would happen. But the next second decided it.

Diving out of the sky, guns full on, machine guns hammering, a squadron of sleek Italian fighters lanced upon them. Bullets scattered dust in a line of geysers. A small bomb exploded.

The officer, Singer and Colter dived for the trench. Another bomb dropped. Machine guns began to hammer from the ground. Rifles racketed. The motors shook the ear with their upclimbing snarls.

And then the ships were gone, racing deeper into the desert, bent on some other mission.

Men came straggling out of the trench, dragging a ragged tatter of a man who now had but half a head. Another bloody corpse was sprawled over the parapet.

All eyes turned wickedly upon the Americans.

"See?" yelled the officer, jabbing his pistol into Colter's stomach. "See? They do not even respect their fellows. They kill everything in sight! They have no heart!"

Colter waited with a bleak expression on his face. The soldiers jumped about brandishing their rifles, shouting in a mighty discord. Singer clutched his DeVry and said nothing.

"You are spies!" cried the officer, "and as spies I am going to shoot you."

"What did he say?" asked Singer in English.

"He said he was going to shoot us," replied Colter. "And these devils look like they mean it, too. Can't say as I blame them."

"Can't say that I . . . Good God, man, are you crazy?"

The fellow with the lion's tail grabbed Colter's arms. Another snatched at Singer. A few turns of a belt and they were unable to move their hands. Without ceremony they were backed up against the parapet.

The Ethiopians, fire added to their anger by the sight of those two mangled bodies, drew off to a range of fifty feet.

"The whole bunch is going to fire," said Colter. "It'll be quick and certain, anyway."

Singer gazed longingly at his camera dropped in the dust. "What a picture *this* would make."

"Wait!" yelled Colter. *"Fermate!"*

The officer stopped backing. "Well?"

"Listen. What will you do with that plane? The Emperor would be angry if he knew that you let a good ship pass through your hands."

"That is true," said the officer, coming closer again. Then he stopped and shook his head. "Bah! You only want to live."

"Listen," said Colter. "I will fix it and fly you to Addis Ababa. You will be promoted."

"I cannot leave my post."

"Send another man. Send that fellow with the lion tail. Tell him to shoot if we head for the Italian lines."

The officer turned to the tall black and after a few words the man began to grin and nod.

The officer gave a command and the belts were removed from the Americans. "Fix the plane. The Emperor will attend to shooting you."

Thankfully, Colter walked to the ship. But Singer picked up the camera, laid it on the parapet and began to grind out pictures. When the natives understood, they bothered him not.

In the engine, Colter discovered that the slug had left both oil and gas lines intact, but had struck the distributor, knocking out a handful of wires. Glumly, he began to patch the copper while the soldiers looked on.

"What a hell of a way," thought Colter, "to earn five grand." But he had needed it. He had been living on front alone. What worried him was the fact that the Italian planes had not held their fire on sighting the ship. What did the Italians think?

Now he had to fly to Addis Ababa—if he could make it—and maybe the Emperor would believe him and maybe not. Certainly, it would look strange to have an unmarked ship roaming around the country. To the Ethiopian, it was clear, a plane meant bombs and bombs meant death and to hell with insignia. They had a grudge against any and all pilots, having no ships themselves worth flying.

At last he had the distributor in working order. He pointed to the cockpit and the fellow with the lion tail climbed in, grinning at his comrades. Singer picked up his camera and headed for the roomy rear cockpit, but the officer stopped him.

"What's the matter with this guy?" yelled Singer.

Colter asked the question.

"Why, there is no need for this man to go. We shall keep him here with us, just in case you fail to get to Addis Ababa." The officer nodded sagely.

"He says you've got to stay here."

"Oh, God," moaned Singer, and then, after a moment, "but maybe I can get some swell pictures. Throw me that other roll of film."

There seemed to be no objection to that and Singer was led back into the trench. Colter watched him go. Maybe they'd execute the poor devil, but then there was nothing Colter could do against a company of well-armed men.

"I'll try to get you out when I get to Addis Ababa," called Colter.

"You'd better," Singer replied.

Colter cranked up the engine. Sand flew and the soldiers ducked. The fellow with the lion tail looked rather dazed, but resolute. He clutched an old-model Lebel in his two strong hands.

Colter taxied around into the hot wind. The heat waves writhed like glass snakes dancing. The Waco took off and roared up into the sky. The company on the ground receded to white dots in their trench.

He pushed south through the rough air. Glancing back at his companion he saw no trace of fear. The fellow was sitting composedly, chewing upon a dark twig.

That was the answer to the lack of fear. The twig was khat, a strong drug which made a man fifty feet high and stronger than a rhino, per twig.

Cautiously, Colter began to angle around into the west, hoping to somehow get back to Asmara. From there he could certainly contact Addis Ababa and have Bill Singer released—if Bill Singer was still alive.

Suddenly a hard muzzle slammed into his back. The fellow

with the lion tail shook his woolly head and pointed south. Resignedly, Colter turned in that direction once more. The man knew his direction by the sun.

He began to have his doubts about his reception in Addis Ababa. Even if he contacted the United States legation, the Ethiopian officials might still have their doubts. They seemed hard to convince.

The air was getting rougher. They were passing over a low line of craggy hills from which the wind lift shot up like an express elevator. Colter looked back. His companion was staring fixedly at the ground. "Airsick," guessed Colter.

Once more he began to wheel into the west, hoping for the best. Once more the muzzle prodded him. But this time Colter's smoldering anger exploded. He turned around and glared. He pointed to himself and to the ground, indicating that without a pilot the native would get killed. The fellow grinned and shrugged, pointing at his own chest.

"Good God," said Colter to himself, "I'll have to try that khat myself."

But for that instant the rifle had been lowered. Colter, disregarding the consequences, reached back and twisted the weapon to one side. The fellow rose up in the cockpit, teeth bared, still holding to the rifle.

An air bump hit the ship and sent it skittering sideways. Colter flipped his safety belt open and sprawled back over the turtleback. The native came closer, a knife appearing in his hand.

Colter snatched the wrist and they stayed there, locked, for a space of seconds while the ship yowled unattended through the sky.

Suddenly Colter became aware of a racketing sound close by. He darted a glance to their right and beheld the squadron of Italian ships he had seen earlier. Bearing down upon them full gun, the Italians were bent upon a swift kill.

Forgotten was the native. Colter whirled and snatched at the stick. He sent the Waco into a steep climb, almost a wingover, trying to get out from under the lines of tracer which hemmed them in like jail bars.

The Ethiopian forgot the fight and, grabbing the Lebel, laid it over the turtleback and fired at the lead ship.

"Now we've done it," moaned Colter.

He raised his hands, empty palms to the sky, and flew in a straight line with his knees. The Lebel rapped again. Colter turned and shook his head. The native doubtfully stopped shooting.

The Italian ships drew in close, flanking the Waco. A black-casqued pilot pointed toward the north. Colter lowered his hands and banked in that direction. The fellow with the lion tail seemed to understand and sat resignedly.

They flew with their forced escort until a rough square of land, presided over by a windsock, appeared below. Then the leader's gesture clearly indicated that they were to land.

Colter went around into the wind and slid down. Mechanics came running and the squadron settled on the runway. Before Colter could climb out, an armed guard took the Ethiopian down by force and then waited for him to alight. Colter looked about for an officer, but the pilots were walking away toward a row of tents.

The guard took Colter and the fellow with the lion tail across the sweltering rough field to a tent which was marked by an Italian flag. The pilots were there, delivering their report. When they came out, they paused and coolly surveyed Colter. Then they shrugged and went on their way.

Inside, Colter was faced with a narrow-eyed, black-mustached Italian major, who rubbed well-kept hands together and said, "So they have an air force now. *Che peccato!* So much more work for us, I suppose."

Colter, aware of the fellow with the lion tail who stood just behind him, said, "No, you do not understand, Major. I am a private pilot flying out of Asmara. This morning I took a World Newsreel cameraman over the border for some actual fighting shots and we were shot down by Ethiopians. He is still there, but—"

"Hah! *Che peccato!* What a pity. I am afraid that I cannot believe you. You have a rifleman here and you were flying south, deeper into Ethiopia, probably returning to Addis Ababa. You are, quite obviously, a misguided American serving with the Ethiopians. But if you are, then you are not in uniform. How do I know that you are not a spy? Perhaps this other man is a pilot you have trained. Perhaps you were to be landed within our lines and he was to return the ship. Yes, that is it."

"Please," said Colter, handing over his papers. *"Ho una lettera. . . ."*

The major glanced at them with bad temper born of excessive heat and worry.

"Forged, all forged. Bah! You are a spy without any doubt whatever. But to be certain, I shall communicate with headquarters by radio. I should have an answer sometime tonight."

He began to write the message and although Colter was hard put to read the thing upside down, he read, "Have apprehended suspicious soldier from enemy lines. Claims he is noncombatant. Fired upon our planes in capture. Have reason to believe he is a spy. Awaiting orders."

"But," cried Colter, "you haven't even mentioned my name!"

"What is it?"

"Colter. Larry Colter."

"Lahray. All right, I'll put it in."

"But that isn't the way you spell it!"

"It's close enough and it's too damned hot to bother. Guard! Take him away!"

Colter and the Ethiopian were dragged off to an isolated tent. Colter was raging but it did him no good. The fellow with the lion tail was stolid.

They were placed in the sweltering tent and they could see the shadow of the guard who stood outside with a fixed bayonet. The Ethiopian stretched out on the rocky ground and promptly went to sleep. But it was too hot for that, according to Colter's way of thinking. He stripped off his shirt and fanned away the settling flies with it.

The Ethiopian snored and Colter swore in a weary

monotone. He was certain of his fate. An order would come back to execute him and that would be that. But you couldn't exactly blame the major. The man was out of his head with the heat and the filth and the terrific job which faced him.

The major with his handful of planes had to patrol a land where a forced landing meant death. Colter's experience had proven that. And the targets out there were elusive, to say the least. Yes, the major had a big job, and spies were probably too numerous to mention due to the raggedness of the fighting lines. One hundred and sixty degrees was rather common in the region and what temper could stand that?

And every time Colter went over the facts he would explode again. The fellow with the lion tail, however, slept peacefully, flies going in and out of his open mouth.

At sunset a *soldato* came with a pannikin of water and a plate of nondescript food. Colter drank and let the native do the eating. The water was full of swimming things but it tasted remarkably good.

Night brought an abrupt coolness and Colter put his shirt back on. About nine o'clock a lantern was thrust into the tent and the major's mustachios twitched over the yellow glare.

"Oh, still here?" said the major. "You want to give me any data on Addis Ababa and this flying force that seems to be organizing?"

"I tell you," began Colter, "that I'm from Asmara—"

"Oh, well, if that's the way it is. The radio came back. They know of no Lahray in Asmara. They said to get rid of you." The major paused for a moment and then said, "I can't understand it at all," and went away.

Colter scowled into the blackness for a long time. Funny nobody in Asmara had connected this up. But then Singer had not known exactly when they would get back, or if they'd return straight to Asmara.

Poor Singer. Those devils had probably executed him by this time. And it wouldn't be long before a firing squad would execute Larry Colter.

At midnight the fellow with the lion tail nudged Colter, and taking his hand, guided it to a knife the native had evidently hidden away in his cotton garments. The touch of cold steel was gruesome. It was a little lighter in the tent now that the moon had risen. Colter saw the Ethiopian's teeth flash in a broad smile.

The fellow went to the rear of the tent and very silently began to cut a slit, a thread at a time. It took almost half an hour to make a hole big enough for a man to squeeze through. The black slid out like a snake.

Colter saw the shadow of the guard against the inside of the canvas. He saw a dark blot appear beside it. Then the guard's shadow slid slowly down and out of sight. The other crept back.

"It was time," thought Colter, "to go." He scrambled through the slit and met the Ethiopian who clutched a new Italian rifle. The Ethiopian looked fixedly at him and then, with apparent decision, slung the rifle and whisked out the stained knife. The man pointed out at the flying field which was bathed in a milky murk under a sliver of a moon.

Colter marched. The native was chewing another twig of khat produced from nowhere and this was certainly no place to start an argument, especially when you couldn't talk the language of a man.

The native's white cotton shirt showed up plainly, but no concern showed on the dark face. Quite boldly, he marched his captive toward the line of planes.

Colter tried to walk slowly but he wanted to run and run fast. Any moment would find them discovered, any moment would send ribbons of flame lancing at them from across the field.

But they walked.

He could see his Waco standing unattended along with the rest. Where were the guards?

They came within ten feet of the ship before they detected any movement about it. A sentry walked forth without any alarm. It came to Colter then that the sight of a native was not uncommon here. Natives were also in the ranks of Italy. And in his dark khaki, Colter might be mistaken for an officer.

The knife prodded him on, straight toward the soldier. Was this fellow with the lion's tail completely insane?

Colter lifted his chin and narrowed the distance. The sentry, quite as a matter of form, lifted his rifle to port and started to challenge them. Then the Italian's expression changed. He opened his mouth to shout.

Colter swung out with his fist. His knuckles crunched against the soldier's jaw. The soldier went down. Colter leaped over the man and raced for the cockpit of his plane. The native hammered hard on his heels and vaulted into the rear pit.

Colter swung the club. The engine caught and bellowed loud enough to wake every man in Africa. Guards came tumbling from everywhere. Colter jumped into his pit and shoved his throttle all the way forward. Pistols flashed, rifles cracked and the Waco gathered momentum down the runway.

Other planes sputtered into life on the line. Other pilots were rushing down the runway.

Colter yanked his ship off and climbed fast. He knew that he was no match for a pursuit ship, either in rate of climb or speed, but he had to make some effort.

A thousand feet leaped away from them and then another thousand. The red fire of exhaust stacks flared below. Above, the slit of a moon floated in its blue-white inverted bowl.

The dagger prodded Colter sharply in the back and a white-clad arm was pointing south again. Colter sent the Waco streaking through the murk, looking anxiously back at the following pursuit planes.

He changed his course a few degrees, hiding his own exhaust stack. The fellow with the lion tail did not seem to mind.

Three ships were hanging on, lower, but coming fast. Colter began to have regrets about the photographic expedition. He was in no position to fight back and the thought galled him. And even if he did fight back there might be grave consequences with Italy—that is, if he lived through it.

A range of hills was just ahead, ragged against the luminous horizon. Colter put the Waco into a steep dive. The pursuit planes were coming within shooting distance. The hills became suddenly distinct.

A ravine, black-floored and yawning, opened up just ahead. Colter raced for it. His power dive gave him more speed.

*Three ships were hanging on, lower, but coming fast. Colter
began to have regrets about the photographic expedition.
He was in no position to fight back and the thought galled him.*

The canyon edges folded over his wings and the roaring engine trebled in volume.

He flew down the long slash, turning with it, engulfed by it. He came to another and cocked his wings at five o'clock. Another and another bank.

A blank wall faced him. He hauled back on the stick and sent his plane rocketing up, hanging on its prop. The edge scraped and almost rolled his wheels.

And then they were flying free without any trace of pursuit whatever. Colter started to sag back in his pit for a well-earned rest.

The knife prodded him again.

The fellow with the lion tail was pointing out their course again. "What was this guy?" thought Colter. "A homing pigeon?"

The knife jabbed again, insistently, rather harder than necessary. Colter felt the oozing of blood down his back. The white-clad arm was pointing down.

Surprised, he saw that they had come back to the entrenchment they had seen earlier in the day. The trench itself stretched like a pencil mark on the whitish ground.

Colter sized up the landing field, remembered his wind direction and came down for a three-point.

White ghosts swarmed out to meet them. The officer came first, automatic in hand, shouting angrily at the fellow with the lion tail.

"Oh God," thought Colter, "it's all over now. This officer wouldn't risk it again. He'd do the shooting without further argument."

Rifles gleamed, teeth gleamed, white shirts milled about. Colter, at yet another prod from the knife, shut off the engine and wearily climbed out. No matter how bad he'd needed that five grand, he needed it no more. It was all over but the shooting.

Singer was nowhere to be seen and Colter thought the worst.

But the big fellow with the lion tail was starting to shout and gesticulate and move back and forth excitedly as he talked. He shook the new rifle and rattled the new bandolier. He pointed at the plane, the sky, straight down. He rolled his eyes. He yelled.

And the Ethiopians stood about with open mouths, staring at Colter and the big fellow.

The officer began to relax. He put away the automatic. The big fellow continued his story at great length with many, many gestures.

But Colter saw nothing funny in it. He scowled, uncomprehending. He was more worried about Singer than anything else.

"Listen," said Colter to the officer, "where is the other man?"

Impatiently, still listening to the big fellow, Dejazwach said, "The other? He's been shot." And then he nodded his head as the man with the lion tail talked on.

Colter's heart turned upside down. He stared at these men, tried to comprehend his own position there, and suddenly his anger, mounting gradually through the day, exploded in red flame.

The big fellow was the nearest to him. Colter reached out

and grabbed the man's arms. The native, surprised, whirled aside and tried to raise the dagger he still carried. Colter wrenched the weapon free and sent it spinning. Colter drove the rifle away.

The big fellow, gathering his wits, reached out with his mighty arms and tried to catch Colter in his grasp. Colter backed up, stepped in and slammed a hard right into the other's jaw. He followed it with a left to the breadbasket, another to the jaw.

The big fellow staggered. Colter waded in, all control gone. Might as well die fighting. Might as well have it out for those knife gashes in his back.

He landed blow after blow and the ring of warriors widened about them. Their small blue shadows weaved under the slit of a moon and the dust rose up unseen to choke them.

The big fellow went down. Colter landed on top of him and grabbed for the throat. His fingers sank deep into the man's windpipe.

Suddenly hands pried them apart. Colter tried to squirm away but a half-dozen men were holding him.

The big fellow stood up, dizzily, swaying back and forth and spitting blood. He looked for a long time at Colter. Then he began to smile with a flash of even white teeth. Colter, seeing nothing funny in it, swore.

The big fellow walked slowly forward, picking up his dagger and rifle as he came. "It was all over now," thought Colter. The warriors held him solid in their grasp. It would be simple to slit his throat.

Abruptly, the man with the lion tail put away his dagger and held out his hand. The men released Colter and, surprised, Colter took the offered palm.

The native said something in Amharic and the officer, smiling, translated it. "He says you are the first man who ever whipped him. He says that you are a great fighter. He says you are his brother."

"What the devil?" said Colter.

"Why, he's been telling us how brave you were. How you charged an Italian plane and forced it to go down in flames. And how he shot down another Italian plane at your orders. And how you were detained in blowing up the enemy airdrome. I realize that he was bragging too much, perhaps, but then . . . well, maybe he did deserve that beating."

Amazed at the turn of things, wanting to laugh now that everything was clear to him, Colter leaned against his ship and looked them over. They were smiling at him.

And then, from the end of the trench hobbled Bill Singer, a bandage swathed about his head.

"Hello, you back?" said Singer. "I got knocked on the head. Boy, did we have some air raids over here. Six bombers came down and shot the hell right out of us and I got the whole thing. Bombs dropping, machine guns going . . . everything. I got a graze on the head, that's all. And boy, have I got pictures! Have I got pictures!"

Colter grinned and Singer grinned and the officer grinned and the big fellow grinned. Then Colter looked up at the sky and saw they had plenty of moonlight left.

"Come on, Bill," he said, "we'd better be getting up to Asmara. If we fly high and fast, we won't be spotted."

They shook hands all around and Singer loaded his camera and precious film. When he climbed into the cockpit Singer said, "This film is great stuff, I'm telling you. It's worth big money to the outfit. I'll put a twenty percent bonus on that five grand, Larry."

Colter nodded and started the engine. He eased into the pit and shook hands all around again.

"We'll have to do this again real soon," chirped Bill Singer. "Boy, have I got pictures!"

"Not for any price," said Colter. "When I'm in a war, I don't like to have to fight both sides. I like an army with me, too. I guess these armies get awful jealous of their wars—they're so hard to find these days."

And they took off and flew high and went straight to Asmara where the papers said that an Ethiopian air attack had been staged on the frontier, that an infamous international spy had been shot at the border, and that Italian planes had killed fifteen thousand men, women and children after a terrific battle at a certain post supposed to be commanded by General Dejazwach.

Story Preview

NOW that you've just ventured through some of the captivating tales in the Stories from the Golden Age collection by L. Ron Hubbard, turn the page and enjoy a preview of *The Dive Bomber*. Join famous test pilot Lucky Martin when he clashes with a man who wants to sell planes to a foreign power and will stop at nothing—including sabotage—to destroy Martin and double-cross the US government.

The Dive Bomber

L UCKY looked sideways to find a man who was as tall as he was but who weighed at least two hundred pounds more. Bullard's fat looked like it had been hung on him roll by roll. His brows bulged over small, quick eyes. His jaw protruded loosely, hiding his collar and tie. His paunch looked as though he had moored a blimp to his belt and let some of the helium out. A giant who rumbled rather than talked, who grinned eternally, Bullard possessed a heartiness which was too studied to be casual.

"Hello," said Lucky, looking back up at the ship.

"The great Lucky Martin," said Bullard, taking the pilot's hard palm in the fat folds of his own and shaking it. "Well, this is a pleasure. I hear you're to be the next boss in case anything happens. . . ."

Lucky looked steadily into the shifty eyes. "What did you say?"

"I said you're sure Lucky, you sure deserve that name. Is this the pretty lady you're going to marry? Well, well, Lucky is putting it much too mild. Always good politics to marry the daughter of . . ."

The crack of Lucky's backhand against the fat mouth jarred the otherwise silent field.

Bullard's eyes glowed redly, but he grinned and bowed and scraped. "I didn't mean any harm, Mr. Martin. I'm sorry I said it, though it did . . ."

"He's coming down!" yelled a mechanic named Lefty Flynn.

Forgotten was Bullard. The song of the dive bomber's engine had been a soft whisper before. Now the sound began to rise in pitch and volume, to a hoarse roar, upward to a rasping snarl, and higher still to a shrill, hammering scream which stabbed down and bludgeoned the field.

The dive bomber had gone over the hump. Nose pointing straight at the earth, eighteen thousand feet down, engine on full, building up to terminal velocity when the resistance of the wind equaled the downward drive of the wide-open throttle.

From a dot against the blue, the ship swiftly became a silver cross inverted. Larger and larger, doubling in size with each passing second, the plane was hurling itself toward the checkerboard of earth, to seemingly certain destruction.

But this was not dangerous. The buildings shook with the flood of sound, ears deafened and closed. But this was not the worst. In a moment O'Neal would pull out and then the danger would come.

To jerk a ship level from a downward speed of seven miles a minute or more would put a strain of nine times the plane's weight on the wings. From two hundred pounds, the pilot's weight would be instantaneously stepped to eighteen hundred pounds, every ounce of which would be bent on crushing him into his pit. Men's brains came loose in their skulls when the pullout was too sharp. Wings came off when the gravity increased to eleven. Over that men became a senseless, bleeding mass, smashed into their cockpit.

"He knows what he's doing," prayed Lucky into the din.

"The ship can take it," whispered Dixie.

Three thousand feet up, still howling straight at the earth, the dive bomber was due to level out.

Lucky would have given ten years of his life to have been in that plane instead of O'Neal. Up there it was too loud and hectic to think. Down here it was terrible.

The plane's nose pulled up slightly, fighting the inertia which strove to dash the silver wings to fragments against the dusty earth.

Abruptly the ship snapped level.

For an instant it sped straight out toward the horizon and then, as though a bomb had exploded between the struts, it flew into countless bits of wreckage which sailed in a scattering cloud about the fuselage.

"Her wings!" yelled Lawson. "Bail out! Good God, he's trapped!"

They could see O'Neal's head. He raised one hand. He strove to pry himself out of the plunging coffin which, with renewed speed was darting straight down again.

He might have made it if he had had another thousand feet.

Belt unbuckled, blasted back against the seat, O'Neal stayed where he was, half out of his pit, until the gleaming fuselage vanished into the earth, leaving a spreading cloud of twisted metal fragments to mingle with the hovering dust.

The silence which ensued was cut only by the soft patter of wreckage settling on the field.

People broke free from the paralysis of horror and began to run toward the plane. The crash siren screamed and an ambulance leaped toward the spot where no ambulance was needed.

Dixie tried to follow but could not. A mechanic's wife gently put her arm across the girl's shoulders and turned her face away from the lazy, curling dust.

Lucky was standing on the edge of the pit, looking down through the smoke. The banks had caved, quenching any fire, burying O'Neal.

Lucky wiped his hands across his face and slid over the shifting clay, searching for the cockpit.

To find out more about *The Dive Bomber* and how you can obtain your copy, go to www.goldenagestories.com.

Glossary

Glossary

STORIES FROM THE GOLDEN AGE *reflect the words and expressions used in the 1930s and 1940s, adding unique flavor and authenticity to the tales. While a character's speech may often reflect regional origins, it also can convey attitudes common in the day. So that readers can better grasp such cultural and historical terms, uncommon words or expressions of the era, the following glossary has been provided.*

Addis Ababa: capital and largest city of Ethiopia. The modern city was founded in 1887 and is located in central Ethiopia. It was given the name Addis Ababa, which means "new flower," by Emperor Menelik II who built his palace there. Since 1889 it has been the capital and residence of the emperor. From May 1936 until it was liberated in May 1941, the city was occupied by the Italian government.

Adwa: town located near the northern border of Ethiopia. In October 1935, Italian troops advanced from Eritrea, which at that time was an Italian colony north of Ethiopia, and captured Adwa.

altimeter: a gauge that measures altitude.

Amharic: the official language of Ethiopia.

ASI: airspeed indicator.

Asmara: largest city and capital of Eritrea, an independent state in East Africa. Eritrea is bounded on the east by the Red Sea, on the south and west by Ethiopia and on the north by Sudan. First established in 1890, Eritrea was an Italian colony between 1890 and 1941.

attack: attack aircraft; a high-speed military or naval airplane designed to destroy enemy aircraft in the air.

bandolier: a broad belt worn over the shoulder by soldiers and having a number of small loops or pockets for holding cartridges.

bolívars: coins and the monetary unit of Venezuela.

Bristol: two-seater fighter biplane of World War I, manufactured by the British and flown by the Royal Air Force until 1932.

camera guns: aircraft-mounted motion picture cameras that record the firing of the guns and their target line as aimed by the pilot.

casqued: wearing a helmet-shaped head covering.

caterpillar: a member of the Caterpillar Club, those who have successfully used a parachute to bail out of a disabled aircraft. The name "Caterpillar Club" makes reference to the silk threads that made the original parachutes, thus recognizing the debt owed to the silkworm and the fact that the caterpillar lets itself down to earth by a silken thread. "Life depends on a silken thread" is the club's motto.

Chaco: the Chaco War (1932–1935) was a border dispute fought between Bolivia and Paraguay over control of a great part of the Gran Chaco region of South America, which was incorrectly thought to be rich in oil.

Che peccato!: (Italian) What a pity!

Chiang: Chiang Kei-shek (1887–1975); served as leader of the Chinese Nationalist Party after the death of its founder in 1925. In 1927 civil war broke out between the Nationalist government and the Red Army led by Mao Tse-tung. In 1934, Chiang surrounded the Communists, but they broke out and began their Great Heroic Trek. In 1949 the Communists gained control of the Chinese mainland and Chiang retreated to Taiwan where he established a government in exile.

club: airplane propeller.

coup de grâce: (French) a finishing stroke.

cowl: the removable metal housing of an aircraft engine, often designed as part of the airplane's body, containing the cockpit, passenger seating and cargo but excluding the wings.

CPVAJRA: Chinese People's Vanguard Anti-Japanese Red Army.

crate: an airplane.

Datemi un tubo per la benzina: (Italian) Give me a hose for gasoline.

dear dead days: nostalgia, a sentimental longing for the past, typically for a period or place with happy personal associations. The phrase comes from the first line in "Love's Old Sweet Song" written in 1884 by J. Clifton Bingham.

DeVry: manufacturer of 35mm and 16mm movie cameras popular in the 1930s, especially with newsreel cameramen.

dixie: a mess tin or oval pot often used in camp for cooking or boiling (as tea).

Ethiopian War: war waged between Italy and Ethiopia from 1935 until 1941. In the early 1930s Italy controlled Eritrea and Somalia, two African nations that border Ethiopia on the north, east and southeast. After negotiations between the governments of Italy and Ethiopia broke down, Italian troops invaded Ethiopia in the north and captured the town of Adwa, which marked the start of the war.

Fermate!: (Italian) Stop!

firewall: a barrier between the engine and cockpit in the event of an engine fire. It helps keep the people in the cockpit from becoming engulfed in flames while flying.

flying kit: outfit necessary for flying, including flying suit, boots, scarf, goggles and helmet.

fotografo, un: (Italian) a photographer.

G: gravity; a unit of acceleration equal to the acceleration of gravity at the Earth's surface.

gibbet: an upright post with a crosspiece, forming a T-shaped structure from which criminals were formerly hanged for public viewing.

G-men: government men; agents of the Federal Bureau of Investigation.

greaseballs: workers who lubricate the working parts of a machine or vehicle.

Great God Bud: Buddha; line from the poem "Mandalay" by Rudyard Kipling.

Great Heroic Trek: also known as the Long March. In October 1934, the Communists, under the command of

Mao Tse-tung, escaped annihilation by Chiang Kai-shek's troops by retreating 8,000 miles (12,500 km) from southern China to Shensi over 370 days. The route passed through some of the most difficult terrain of China and the march was completed by only one-tenth of the force that started.

Greek Rebellion: Greco-Turkish War (1919–1922); war between Greece and Turkish revolutionaries. After World War I, the territories and peoples formerly under the Turkish Empire were divided into various new nations and territories. The Greek campaign was launched because western allies had promised Greece territorial gains at the expense of the Turkish Empire. It ended with Greece giving up all territory gained during the war, returning to its prewar borders.

ground loop: to cause an aircraft to ground loop, or make a sharp horizontal turn when taxiing, landing or taking off.

gun: throttle.

hit the silk: parachute from an aircraft; bail out.

hoodoo: one that brings bad luck.

Ho una lettera: (Italian) I have a letter.

Inner Mongolia: an autonomous region of northeast China. Originally the southern section of Mongolia, it was annexed by China in 1635, later becoming an integral part of China in 1911.

Io sono Dejazwach: (Italian) I am Dejazwach.

khat: a flowering plant native to tropical East Africa. It is a shrub or small tree with evergreen leaves, and contains an amphetamine-like stimulant that causes excitement and euphoria. The ancient Egyptians considered the khat plant a "divine food" and used the plant as a metamorphic process to transcend to a divine level, intending to make the user godlike.

lanyard: a cord attached to a cannon's trigger mechanism, which when pulled, fires the cannon.

Lebels: French rifles that were adopted as standard infantry weapons in 1887 and remained in official service until after World War II.

Lewis: a gas-operated machine gun designed by US Army Colonel Isaac Newton Lewis in 1911. The gun weighed twenty-eight pounds, only about half as much as a typical medium machine gun. The lightness of the gun made it popular as an aircraft-mounted weapon, especially since the cooling effect of the high-speed air over the gun meant that the gun's cooling mechanisms could be removed, making the weapon even lighter.

mags: magnetos; small ignition system devices that use permanent magnets to generate a spark in internal combustion engines, especially in marine and aircraft engines.

Mannlicher: a type of rifle equipped with a manually operated sliding bolt for loading cartridges for firing, as opposed to the more common rotating bolt of other rifles. Mannlicher rifles were considered reasonably strong and accurate.

Mao: Mao Tse-tung (1893–1976); Chinese leader of the Communist Party of China, who defeated the Chinese Nationalist Party led by Chiang Kai-shek in the Chinese Civil War (1927–1950).

more's the pity: sadly, unfortunately.

mushy stall: a situation in which the controls of an aircraft are sluggish or feel mushy and it is difficult to precisely control the plane. This is an indicator that the plane is in a stall or is about to stall. This can occur when the airspeed goes below what is needed for the airplane to maintain altitude.

Newton: Sir Isaac Newton (1643–1727); English mathematician and physicist. Famous for his laws of motion, which are laws concerning the relations between force, motion, acceleration, mass and inertia, and that govern the motion of material objects.

orderly sergeant: the first sergeant of a company whose duties formerly included the conveyance of orders.

palm grease: a bribe.

pannikin: a small metal drinking cup.

Parlate Italiano?: (Italian) Do you speak Italian?

pyrene: fire extinguisher fluid.

quirt: a riding whip with a short handle and a braided leather lash.

ring: release ring on a parachute, which when pulled releases and unfolds the parachute.

rip cord: a cord on a parachute that, when pulled, opens the parachute for descent.

Rolls: an aircraft engine built by Rolls-Royce, a British car and aero-engine manufacturing company founded in 1906.

rowels: the small spiked revolving wheels on the ends of spurs, which are attached to the heels of a rider's boots and used to nudge a horse into going faster.

rudder: a device used to steer ships or aircraft. A rudder is a flat plane or sheet of material attached with hinges to the craft's stern or tail. In typical aircraft, pedals operate rudders via mechanical linkages.

Scheherazade: the female narrator of *The Arabian Nights*, who during one thousand and one adventurous nights saved her life by entertaining her husband, the king, with stories.

Shanghai: city of eastern China at the mouth of the Yangtze River, and the largest city in the country. Shanghai was opened to foreign trade by treaty in 1842 and quickly prospered. France, Great Britain and the United States all held large concessions (rights to use land granted by a government) in the city until the early twentieth century.

Shensi: a province of east central China; one of the earliest cultural and political centers of China and site of the conclusion of the Great Heroic Trek (also known as the Long March).

shrouds: the ropes connecting the harness and canopy of a parachute.

slip: (of an aircraft when excessively banked) to slide sideways, toward the center of the curve described in turning.

slipstream: the airstream pushed back by a revolving aircraft propeller.

Snider: a rifle formerly used in the British service. It was invented by American Jacob Snider in the mid-1800s. The Snider was a breech-loading rifle, derived from its muzzle-loading predecessor called the Enfield.

soldato: (Italian) soldier.

struts: supports for a structure such as an aircraft wing, roof or bridge.

tach: tachometer; a device used to determine speed of rotation, typically of an engine's crankshaft, usually measured in revolutions per minute.

terminal velocity: the constant speed that a falling object reaches when the downward gravitational force equals the frictional resistance of the medium through which it is falling, usually air.

three-point: three-point landing; an airplane landing in which the two main wheels and the nose wheel all touch the ground simultaneously.

tracer: a bullet or shell whose course is made visible by a trail of flames or smoke, used to assist in aiming.

trident: a three-lever throttle in a plane. When the lever is pushed forward, it opens the throttle and increases the speed of the plane.

turtleback: the part of the airplane behind the cockpit that is shaped like the back of a turtle.

volley fire: simultaneous artillery fire in which each piece is fired a specified number of rounds without regard to the other pieces, and as fast as accuracy will permit.

Waco: one of a range of civilian biplanes produced by the Weaver Aircraft Company of Ohio (WACO) from 1919 until the company stopped production in 1946. Waco biplanes were known to be reliable and rugged and were popular amongst traveling businessmen, postal services and explorers.

whipstall: a maneuver in a small aircraft in which it goes into a vertical climb, pauses briefly, and then drops toward the earth, nose first.

windsock: a fabric tube or cone attached at one end to the top of a pole to show which way the wind is blowing.

wingover: also known as the Immelmann turn; an aerial maneuver named after World War I flying ace Max Immelmann. The pilot pulls the aircraft into a vertical climb, applying full rudder as the speed drops, then rolls the aircraft while pulling back slightly on the stick, causing the aircraft to dive back down in the opposite direction. It has become one of the most popular aerial maneuvers in the world.

wings and bars: insignia consisting of a pair of wings with an anchor worn by qualified naval aviators. The bars are the insignia of a lieutenant in the navy consisting of two medium gold stripes (bars).

Yellow River: the second longest river in China, flowing through the north central part of the country.

L. Ron Hubbard
in the Golden Age
of Pulp Fiction

*In writing an adventure story
a writer has to know that he is adventuring
for a lot of people who cannot.
The writer has to take them here and there
about the globe and show them
excitement and love and realism.
As long as that writer is living the part of an
adventurer when he is hammering
the keys, he is succeeding with his story.*

*Adventuring is a state of mind.
If you adventure through life, you have a
good chance to be a success on paper.*

*Adventure doesn't mean globe-trotting,
exactly, and it doesn't mean great deeds.
Adventuring is like art.
You have to live it to make it real.*

—*L. RON HUBBARD*

L. Ron Hubbard
and American
Pulp Fiction

B ORN March 13, 1911, L. Ron Hubbard lived a life at
least as expansive as the stories with which he enthralled
a hundred million readers through a fifty-year career.

Originally hailing from Tilden, Nebraska, he spent his
formative years in a classically rugged Montana, replete with
the cowpunchers, lawmen and desperadoes who would later
people his Wild West adventures. And lest anyone imagine
those adventures were drawn from vicarious experience, he
was not only breaking broncs at a tender age, he was also
among the few whites ever admitted into Blackfoot society
as a bona fide blood brother. While if only to round out an
otherwise rough and tumble youth, his mother was that rarity
of her time—a thoroughly educated woman—who introduced
her son to the classics of Occidental literature even before his
seventh birthday.

But as any dedicated L. Ron Hubbard reader will attest, his
world extended far beyond Montana. In point of fact, and as the
son of a United States naval officer, by the age of eighteen he
had traveled over a quarter of a million miles. Included therein
were three Pacific crossings to a then still mysterious Asia, where
he ran with the likes of Her British Majesty's agent-in-place

L. Ron Hubbard, left, at Congressional Airport, Washington, DC, 1931, with members of George Washington University flying club.

for North China, and the last in the line of Royal Magicians from the court of Kublai Khan. For the record, L. Ron Hubbard was also among the first Westerners to gain admittance to forbidden Tibetan monasteries below Manchuria, and his photographs of China's Great Wall long graced American geography texts.

Upon his return to the United States and a hasty completion of his interrupted high school education, the young Ron Hubbard entered George Washington University. There, as fans of his aerial adventures may have heard, he earned his wings as a pioneering barnstormer at the dawn of American aviation. He also earned a place in free-flight record books for the longest sustained flight above Chicago. Moreover, as a roving reporter for *Sportsman Pilot* (featuring his first professionally penned articles), he further helped inspire a generation of pilots who would take America to world airpower.

Immediately beyond his sophomore year, Ron embarked on the first of his famed ethnological expeditions, initially to then untrammeled Caribbean shores (descriptions of which would later fill a whole series of West Indies mystery-thrillers). That the Puerto Rican interior would also figure into the future of Ron Hubbard stories was likewise no accident. For in addition to cultural studies of the island, a 1932–33

LRH expedition is rightly remembered as conducting the first complete mineralogical survey of a Puerto Rico under United States jurisdiction.

There was many another adventure along this vein: As a lifetime member of the famed Explorers Club, L. Ron Hubbard charted North Pacific waters with the first shipboard radio direction finder, and so pioneered a long-range navigation system universally employed until the late twentieth century. While not to put too fine an edge on it, he also held a rare Master Mariner's license to pilot any vessel, of any tonnage in any ocean.

Yet lest we stray too far afield, there is an LRH note at this juncture in his saga, and it reads in part:

"I started out writing for the pulps, writing the best I knew, writing for every mag on the stands, slanting as well as I could."

To which one might add: His earliest submissions date from the summer of 1934, and included tales drawn from true-to-life Asian adventures, with characters roughly modeled on British/American intelligence operatives he had known in Shanghai. His early Westerns were similarly peppered with details drawn from personal

Capt. L. Ron Hubbard in Ketchikan, Alaska, 1940, on his Alaskan Radio Experimental Expedition, the first of three voyages conducted under the Explorers Club flag.

experience. Although therein lay a first hard lesson from the often cruel world of the pulps. His first Westerns were soundly rejected as lacking the authenticity of a Max Brand yarn (a particularly frustrating comment given L. Ron Hubbard's Westerns came straight from his Montana homeland, while Max Brand was a mediocre New York poet named Frederick Schiller Faust, who turned out implausible six-shooter tales from the terrace of an Italian villa).

Nevertheless, and needless to say, L. Ron Hubbard persevered and soon earned a reputation as among the most publishable names in pulp fiction, with a ninety percent placement rate of first-draft manuscripts. He was also among the most prolific, averaging between seventy and a hundred thousand words a month. Hence the rumors that L. Ron Hubbard had redesigned a typewriter for faster keyboard action and pounded out manuscripts on a continuous roll of butcher paper to save the precious seconds it took to insert a single sheet of paper into manual typewriters of the day.

That all L. Ron Hubbard stories did not run beneath said byline is yet another aspect of pulp fiction lore. That is, as publishers periodically rejected manuscripts from top-drawer authors if only to avoid paying top dollar, L. Ron Hubbard and company just as frequently replied with submissions under various pseudonyms. In Ron's case, the list

---

A MAN OF MANY NAMES

Between 1934 and 1950, L. Ron Hubbard authored more than fifteen million words of fiction in more than two hundred classic publications. To supply his fans and editors with stories across an array of genres and pulp titles, he adopted fifteen pseudonyms in addition to his already renowned L. Ron Hubbard byline.

Winchester Remington Colt
Lt. Jonathan Daly
Capt. Charles Gordon
Capt. L. Ron Hubbard
Bernard Hubbel
Michael Keith
Rene Lafayette
Legionnaire 148
Legionnaire 14830
Ken Martin
Scott Morgan
Lt. Scott Morgan
Kurt von Rachen
Barry Randolph
Capt. Humbert Reynolds

---

included: Rene Lafayette, Captain Charles Gordon, Lt. Scott Morgan and the notorious Kurt von Rachen—supposedly on the lam for a murder rap, while hammering out two-fisted prose in Argentina. The point: While L. Ron Hubbard as Ken Martin spun stories of Southeast Asian intrigue, LRH as Barry Randolph authored tales of romance on the Western range—which, stretching between a dozen genres is how he came to stand among the two hundred elite authors providing close to a million tales through the glory days of American Pulp Fiction.

L. Ron Hubbard, circa 1930, at the outset of a literary career that would finally span half a century.

In evidence of exactly that, by 1936 L. Ron Hubbard was literally leading pulp fiction's elite as president of New York's American Fiction Guild. Members included a veritable pulp hall of fame: Lester "Doc Savage" Dent, Walter "The Shadow" Gibson, and the legendary Dashiell Hammett—to cite but a few.

Also in evidence of just where L. Ron Hubbard stood within his first two years on the American pulp circuit: By the spring of 1937, he was ensconced in Hollywood, adopting a Caribbean thriller for Columbia Pictures, remembered today as *The Secret of Treasure Island.* Comprising fifteen thirty-minute episodes, the L. Ron Hubbard screenplay led to the most profitable matinée serial in Hollywood history. In accord with Hollywood culture, he was thereafter continually called

The 1937 Secret of Treasure Island, *a fifteen-episode serial adapted for the screen by L. Ron Hubbard from his novel,* Murder at Pirate Castle.

upon to rewrite/doctor scripts—most famously for long-time friend and fellow adventurer Clark Gable.

In the interim—and herein lies another distinctive chapter of the L. Ron Hubbard story—he continually worked to open Pulp Kingdom gates to up-and-coming authors. Or, for that matter, anyone who wished to write. It was a fairly unconventional stance, as markets were already thin and competition razor sharp. But the fact remains, it was an L. Ron Hubbard hallmark that he vehemently lobbied on behalf of young authors—regularly supplying instructional articles to trade journals, guest-lecturing to short story classes at George Washington University and Harvard, and even founding his own creative writing competition. It was established in 1940, dubbed the Golden Pen, and guaranteed winners both New York representation and publication in *Argosy*.

But it was John W. Campbell Jr.'s *Astounding Science Fiction* that finally proved the most memorable LRH vehicle. While every fan of L. Ron Hubbard's galactic epics undoubtedly knows the story, it nonetheless bears repeating: By late 1938, the pulp publishing magnate of Street & Smith was determined to revamp *Astounding Science Fiction* for broader readership. In particular, senior editorial director F. Orlin Tremaine called for stories with a stronger *human element*. When acting editor John W. Campbell balked, preferring his spaceship-driven tales,

Tremaine enlisted Hubbard. Hubbard, in turn, replied with the genre's first truly *character-driven* works, wherein heroes are pitted not against bug-eyed monsters but the mystery and majesty of deep space itself—and thus was launched the Golden Age of Science Fiction.

The names alone are enough to quicken the pulse of any science fiction aficionado, including LRH friend and protégé, Robert Heinlein, Isaac Asimov, A. E. van Vogt and Ray Bradbury. Moreover, when coupled with LRH stories of fantasy, we further come to what's rightly been described as the foundation of every modern tale of horror: L. Ron Hubbard's immortal *Fear*. It was rightly proclaimed by Stephen King as one of the very few works to genuinely warrant that overworked term "classic"—as in: *"This is a classic tale of creeping, surreal menace and horror. . . . This is one of the really, really good ones."*

L. Ron Hubbard, 1948, among fellow science fiction luminaries at the World Science Fiction Convention in Toronto.

To accommodate the greater body of L. Ron Hubbard fantasies, Street & Smith inaugurated *Unknown*—a classic pulp if there ever was one, and wherein readers were soon thrilling to the likes of *Typewriter in the Sky* and *Slaves of Sleep* of which Frederik Pohl would declare: *"There are bits and pieces from Ron's work that became part of the language in ways that very few other writers managed."*

And, indeed, at J. W. Campbell Jr.'s insistence, Ron was regularly drawing on themes from the Arabian Nights and so introducing readers to a world of genies, jinn, Aladdin and Sinbad—all of which, of course, continue to float through cultural mythology to this day.

At least as influential in terms of post-apocalypse stories was L. Ron Hubbard's 1940 *Final Blackout*. Generally acclaimed as the finest anti-war novel of the decade and among the ten best works of the genre ever authored—here, too, was a tale that would live on in ways few other writers

imagined. Hence, the later Robert Heinlein verdict: "Final Blackout *is as perfect a piece of science fiction as has ever been written.*"

Like many another who both lived and wrote American pulp adventure, the war proved a tragic end to Ron's sojourn in the pulps. He served with distinction in four theaters and was highly decorated for commanding corvettes in the North Pacific. He was also grievously wounded in combat, lost many a close friend and colleague and thus resolved to say farewell to pulp fiction and devote himself to what it had supported these many years—namely, his serious research.

Portland, Oregon, 1943; L. Ron Hubbard captain of the US Navy subchaser PC 815.

But in no way was the LRH literary saga at an end, for as he wrote some thirty years later, in 1980:

"Recently there came a period when I had little to do. This was novel in a life so crammed with busy years, and I decided to amuse myself by writing a novel that was pure science fiction."

That work was *Battlefield Earth: A Saga of the Year 3000.* It was an immediate *New York Times* bestseller and, in fact, the first international science fiction blockbuster in decades. It was not, however, L. Ron Hubbard's magnum opus, as that distinction is generally reserved for his next and final work: The 1.2 million word *Mission Earth.*

> **Final Blackout**
> *is as perfect*
> *a piece of*
> *science fiction as*
> *has ever*
> *been written.*
>
> —Robert Heinlein

How he managed those 1.2 million words in just over twelve months is yet another piece of the L. Ron Hubbard legend. But the fact remains, he did indeed author a ten-volume *dekalogy* that lives in publishing history for the fact that each and every volume of the series was also a *New York Times* bestseller.

Moreover, as subsequent generations discovered L. Ron Hubbard through republished works and novelizations of his screenplays, the mere fact of his name on a cover signaled an international bestseller. . . . Until, to date, sales of his works exceed hundreds of millions, and he otherwise remains among the most enduring and widely read authors in literary history. Although as a final word on the tales of L. Ron Hubbard, perhaps it's enough to simply reiterate what editors told readers in the glory days of American Pulp Fiction:

He writes the way he does, brothers, because he's been there, seen it and done it!

THE STORIES FROM THE GOLDEN AGE

Your ticket to adventure starts here with the Stories from the Golden Age collection by master storyteller L. Ron Hubbard. These gripping tales are set in a kaleidoscope of exotic locales and brim with fascinating characters, including some of the most vile villains, dangerous dames and brazen heroes you'll ever get to meet.

The entire collection of over one hundred and fifty stories is being released in a series of eighty books and audiobooks. For an up-to-date listing of available titles, go to www.goldenagestories.com.

AIR ADVENTURE

Arctic Wings
The Battling Pilot
Boomerang Bomber
The Crate Killer
The Dive Bomber
Forbidden Gold
Hurtling Wings
The Lieutenant Takes the Sky

Man-Killers of the Air
On Blazing Wings
Red Death Over China
Sabotage in the Sky
Sky Birds Dare!
The Sky-Crasher
Trouble on His Wings
Wings Over Ethiopia

FAR-FLUNG ADVENTURE

The Adventure of "X"
All Frontiers Are Jealous
The Barbarians
The Black Sultan
Black Towers to Danger
The Bold Dare All
Buckley Plays a Hunch
The Cossack
Destiny's Drum
Escape for Three
Fifty-Fifty O'Brien
The Headhunters
Hell's Legionnaire
He Walked to War
Hostage to Death

Hurricane
The Iron Duke
Machine Gun 21,000
Medals for Mahoney
Price of a Hat
Red Sand
The Sky Devil
The Small Boss of Nunaloha
The Squad That Never Came Back
Starch and Stripes
Tomb of the Ten Thousand Dead
Trick Soldier
While Bugles Blow!
Yukon Madness

SEA ADVENTURE

Cargo of Coffins
The Drowned City
False Cargo
Grounded
Loot of the Shanung
Mister Tidwell, Gunner

The Phantom Patrol
Sea Fangs
Submarine
Twenty Fathoms Down
Under the Black Ensign

TALES FROM THE ORIENT

The Devil—With Wings *Pearl Pirate*
The Falcon Killer *The Red Dragon*
Five Mex for a Million *Spy Killer*
Golden Hell *Tah*
The Green God *The Trail of the Red Diamonds*
Hurricane's Roar *Wind-Gone-Mad*
Inky Odds *Yellow Loot*
Orders Is Orders

MYSTERY

The Blow Torch Murder *The Grease Spot*
Brass Keys to Murder *Killer Ape*
Calling Squad Cars! *Killer's Law*
The Carnival of Death *The Mad Dog Murder*
The Chee-Chalker *Mouthpiece*
Dead Men Kill *Murder Afloat*
The Death Flyer *The Slickers*
Flame City *They Killed Him Dead*

135

FANTASY

Borrowed Glory	*If I Were You*
The Crossroads	*The Last Drop*
Danger in the Dark	*The Room*
The Devil's Rescue	*The Tramp*
He Didn't Like Cats	

SCIENCE FICTION

The Automagic Horse	*A Matter of Matter*
Battle of Wizards	*The Obsolete Weapon*
Battling Bolto	*One Was Stubborn*
The Beast	*The Planet Makers*
Beyond All Weapons	*The Professor Was a Thief*
A Can of Vacuum	*The Slaver*
The Conroy Diary	*Space Can*
The Dangerous Dimension	*Strain*
Final Enemy	*Tough Old Man*
The Great Secret	*240,000 Miles Straight Up*
Greed	*When Shadows Fall*
The Invaders	

WESTERN

The Baron of Coyote River *Man for Breakfast*
Blood on His Spurs *The No-Gun Gunhawk*
Boss of the Lazy B *The No-Gun Man*
Branded Outlaw *The Ranch That No One Would Buy*
Cattle King for a Day *Reign of the Gila Monster*
Come and Get It *Ride 'Em, Cowboy*
Death Waits at Sundown *Ruin at Rio Piedras*
Devil's Manhunt *Shadows from Boot Hill*
The Ghost Town Gun-Ghost *Silent Pards*
Gun Boss of Tumbleweed *Six-Gun Caballero*
Gunman! *Stacked Bullets*
Gunman's Tally *Stranger in Town*
The Gunner from Gehenna *Tinhorn's Daughter*
Hoss Tamer *The Toughest Ranger*
Johnny, the Town Tamer *Under the Diehard Brand*
King of the Gunmen *Vengeance Is Mine!*
The Magic Quirt *When Gilhooly Was in Flower*

137

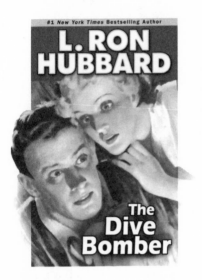

JOIN THE PULP REVIVAL
America in the 1930s and 40s

Pulp fiction was in its heyday and 30 million readers were regularly riveted by the larger-than-life tales of master storyteller L. Ron Hubbard. For this was pulp fiction's golden age, when the writing was raw and every page packed a walloping punch.

That magic can now be yours. An evocative world of nefarious villains, exotic intrigues, courageous heroes and heroines—a world that today's cinema has barely tapped for tales of adventure and swashbucklers.

Enroll today in the Stories from the Golden Age Club and begin receiving your monthly feature edition selected from more than 150 stories in the collection.

You may choose to enjoy them as either a paperback or audiobook for the special membership price of $9.95 each month along with FREE shipping and handling.

CALL TOLL-FREE: 1-877-8GALAXY
(1-877-842-5299) OR GO ONLINE TO
www.goldenagestories.com
AND BECOME PART OF THE PULP REVIVAL!